G. Villers Duke of Buckingham

The works of His Grace George Villiers, Duke of Buckingham

G. Villers Duke of Buckingham

The works of His Grace George Villiers, Duke of Buckingham

ISBN/EAN: 9783743408203

Manufactured in Europe, USA, Canada, Australia, Japa

Cover: Foto ©Andreas Hilbeck / pixelio.de

Manufactured and distributed by brebook publishing software (www.brebook.com)

G. Villers Duke of Buckingham

The works of His Grace George Villiers, Duke of Buckingham

THE
RESTORATION:

OR,

RIGHT WILL TAKE PLACE.

A

TRAGI-COMEDY.

Vol. II.   B

P R O L O G U E.

NOTHING is harder in the world to do,
Than to quit what our nature leads us to.
As this our friend here proves, who, having fpent
His time and wealth for other folks content ;
Tho' he fo much as thanks could never get,
Can't, for his life, quite give it over yet;
But, ftriving ftill to pleafe you, hopes he may,
Without a grievance, try to mend a play.
Perhaps he wifh'd it might have been his fate
To lend a helping hand to mend the ftate:
Tho' he conceives, as things have lately run,
'Tis fomewhat hard at prefent to be done.
Well, let that pafs, the ftars that rule the rout,
Do what we can, I fee, muft whirl about :
But here's the devil on't, that, come what will,
His ftars are fure to make him lofer ftill.
When all the *Polls* together made a din,
Some to put out, and others to put in,
And every where his fellows got and got
From being nothing to be God knows what;
He, for the public, needs would play a game,
For which he has been trounc'd by public fame;
And to fpeak truth, fo he deferv'd to be
For his dull clownifh fingularity :
For when the fafhion is to break one's truft,
'Tis rudenefs then to offer to be juft.

B 2   D R A-

DRAMATIS PERSONÆ.

The King.
Philander, true heir to the crown.
Thrafomond, Prince of Spain.
Cleon, a Lord.
Agremont, } Gentlemen, his confederates,
Adelard,
A Spaniard, Governor to Prince Thrafomond.

W O M E N.

Araminta, the King's daughter.
Melefinda { A modeft lady attending on the Princefs.
Alga, a wanton court lady.
Two other court ladies.
Euphrofyne, { Daughter to Cleon, but difguifed like a page, under the name of Endymion.

Scene, SICILY.

THE

RESTORATION:

OR,

RIGHT WILL TAKE PLACE.

ACT I.   SCENE I.

Cleon, Agremont *and* Adelard.

Agr. HERE'S no body come yet.

Cleon. They had orders from the King to attend here. Befides, it has been publifhed, that no officer fhould deny admiffion to any gentleman that defires to attend and hear.

Agr. Can you guefs the caufe of this ceremony?

Cleon. That's plain, Sir, the foreign Prince that's come to marry Araminta, heirefs to this kingdom.

Adel. Your diving politicians, and thofe who would feem to have deep intelligence, give out that fhe does not like him.

Cleon. O, Sir, the multitude fpeak what they would have. But her father has fent this Prince fo many affurances of the match before his coming over, that I think fhe's refolved to be ruled.

Agr. And will this foreign Prince enjoy both the kingdom of Sicily and Calabria, Sir?

Cleon. That it is fo intended is moft certain; but it will fure be very troublefome and difficult for him to enjoy them both in fafety; the right heir to one of them being now living, and of fo noble and virtuous a character, efpecially when the people are poffeffed with an admiration of the bravery of his mind and pity of his injuries.

Agr. You mean Philander.

Cleon. I mean the fame. His father, we all know, was unjuftly driven by our late King of Ca-labria from his fruitful Sicily: I wifh the blood I drew myfelf in thofe accurfed wars was well wafh'd off.

Agr. My ignorance of the affairs of Sicily will not let me know how it comes to pafs that Philander (being heir to one of thefe kingdoms) the King fhould fuffer him to go abroad fo much at liberty.

Cleon. Your temper is more fortunate, I find, than to bufy yourfelf in enquiring after ftate news; but I muft tell you that lately the King

rifqu'd

rifqu'd both his kingdoms for offering to imprifon Philander. For the city rofe in arms, nor could be quell'd by any threats or force, till they faw the Prince ride thro' the ftreets unguarded; and then throwing up their caps with loud huzzas and bonfires, they laid afide their military appointments. This reafon politicians give for the marriage of his daughter to a foreign Prince, that he may be able to keep his own people in awe by his forces.

Agr. Who is this Prince's father?

Cleon. A perfon of mean extraction, but by wiles and arts obtaining power, ufurp'd the kingdom where he reigns, and keeps it under by a ftanding army, which our King intends to copy.

Enter Melefinda, Alga, *a lady and a Spaniard.*

Adel. See the ladies, what's the firft?

Cleon. A worthy lady that attends the Princefs.

Adel. The other that follows her?

Cleon. She is one that loves to try the feveral conftitutions of mens' bodies, and indeed has deftroyed her own by making experiments upon them, for the good of the commonwealth.

Agr. Of which fhe is certainly a very profitable member.

B 4 . *Adel.*

Adel. And pray what odd grave fellow's that who follows alone?

Cleon. One of Prince Thrafomond's train, and his governour.

Agr. Why? is that Prince a boy?

Cleon. Yes, he's a pretty forward boy about four and twenty.

Adel. That is a forward boy indeed; when will he be a man?

Cleon. Never; he'll live a boy till threefcore, and then turn child again.

May you have your defires, ladies!

Alga. Then you muft fit down by us.

Adel. With all our hearts, ladies.

Gover. I will fit near this lady.

Mel. Not near me, Sir, but there's a lady loves a ftranger, and you appear to me a very ftrange fellow:

Agr. Madam, how ftrange foever he is, he will not be fo long, for I perceive he can quickly be acquainted.

Adel. Peace; the King.

Enter King, Thrafomond, Araminta *and Train.*

King. To give a ftronger teftimony of love
Than only promifes (which commonly

In

In princes find at once both birth and burial)
We've drawn you by our letters, noble Prince,
To make here your addreſſes to our daughter.
And yourſelf known and lov'd by all our ſubjects,
As for this lady maid, whoſe ſex and innocence
Yet teach her nothing but her fears and bluſhes :
I hope her modeſty ſo recommends her to you for
     a wife,
Were ſhe not fair enough to be a miſtreſs.
Laſtly, my noble ſon, (for ſo I now muſt call you)
That I have done this publicly, is not
To add a comfort in particular
To you or me, but all, and to confirm
The nobles and the gentry of theſe kingdoms
By oath to your ſucceſſion ; this ſhall be
Within a week at moſt.
     Adel. This will be hardly done.
     Agr. It muſt be ill done whenſoever it is done.
     Cleon. At leaſt it will be but half done whilſt ſo
brave a man is thrown off and living.

Enter Philander,

Officer. Make room there for the Lord Philander.
Adel. Mark but the King how pale he looks
     with fear,
                                        King,

King. What brings him here? You're curious I find
To fee.this interview.

Phil. The wonders, Sir, your Majefty has often
    fpoken in praife
Of Thrafomond, makes me defire to hear   .
What he can fay himfelf.

Gover. Come, now begin.

Thraf. Kiffing your white hand, miftrefs, I take
    leave
To thank your royal father, and thus far
To be my own free trumpet : then obferve,
Great King, and thefe your fubjeēts, mine that
    muft be.
For fo deferving you have fpoke me, Sir,
(And fo deferving I dare fpeak myfelf)
To a perfon of what eminence,
What expeētation, what faculties,
Manners and virtues you will wed your kingdoms;
You have in me, all you can wifh. This country
By more than all my hopes, I hold moft happy
In their dear memories, that have been kings
Both great and good ; happy in yours, that is,
And from you (as a chronicle to keep
Your noble name from eating age,) do I

                                    Opine

Opine myfelf of all moft happy, Sir.
Believe me in a word, a prince's word,
There fhall be nothing to make up a kingdom
Mighty and flourifhing both fenc'd and fear'd,
But thro' the travels of my life I'll find it,
And tie it to this country : And I vow
My reign fhall be fo eafy to the fubjects,
That every man fhall be his prince himfelf,
And his own law, yet I his prince and law.
And, deareft lady, to your deareft felf ;
Dear in the choice of him, (whofe name and luftre
Muft make you more and mightier,) let me fay,
You are the bleffed'ft living: for, fweet Princefs,
You fhall enjoy a man to be your fervant,
And you fhall make him your's for whom great
            Queens
Muft die and figh.——
    Phil. Thou ugly filly rogue.
    Cleon. I wonder what's his price, for one may fee
He has a mind to fell himfelf by his praifes.
    Agr. Would I might die if I fee any thing
In him to raife him but to a conftable.
    Adel. Now do I fancy that this fpeech was made
        by the governor.
    Agr. O' my confcience I think fo too, for by
                                        his

his action you might fee the fool did not underftand what he faid.

Cleon. Well, we fhall fee more of it anon.

Phil. May I beg leave, Sir, of your Majefty,
To fpeak a word or two with this ftrange prince?

King. I give it you; but ftill remember that you
are a fubject.

Phil. Yes, Sir, I am fo: and more a flave to
· Araminta,
And in fpight of thee and fate will be fo ever. [*Afide.*
Thus—I turn myfelf to you, big foreign man,
Ne'er ftare nor put on wonder, for you muft
Endure me, and you fhall. This earth you tread on
(A dowry, s you hope, with this fair Princefs,
Whofe very name I bow to) was not left
By my dead father (O! I had a father!)
To your inheritance; and I up and living,
Having myfelf about me and my fword,
Thefe arms, and fome few friends befides the gods,
To part fo calmy with it, and fit ftill;
And fay I might have been! I tell thee, Thra-
fomond,
When thou art King, look I be dead and rotten,
And my name loft: hear, hear me, Thrafomond,
This very ground thou go'ft on, this fat earth,

My

My father's friends made fertile with their faith,
Before that day of shame shall gape, and swallow
Thee and thy nation, like a hungry grave,
Into her hidden bowels; Prince, it shall,
By Nemesis it shall.

Cleon. Here's a fellow has some fire in his veins.
The out-landish Prince looks like a tooth-drawer.

King. You do displease us : you're now too bold.

Phil. No, Sir, I am too tame ;
Too much a dove, a thing born without passion ;
A very shadow, that each drunken cloud
Sails over, and makes nothing.

King. What means this ?
Call our physicians ; sure he's somewhat tainted.

Adel. I do not think 'twill prove so.

Cleon. 'Has given him a general purge already,
and now
He means to let him blood. Be constant, gentlemen,
By these hilts I'll run his hazard, tho' I run my
name
Out of the kingdom.

Thras. Must I speak now ?　　[*To his governor.*

Gov. Ay, ay, and do it home.

Thras. What you have seen in me to stir offence
I cannot tell, except it be this lady,
　　　　　　　　　　　　　　　Whom

Whom the king offer'd me without my feeking.
And I expect he will fecure her to me.

Gov You muft be angry, Sir.

Thraf. Well then, I will.———
I value not whofe branch you are, my blood
And perfon do deferve her well, and I
Therefore affure you that fhe fhall be mine.

Phil. If thou were fole inheritor to him
That once fubdu'd the world, and could'ft fee no fun
Shine upon any thing but thine; were Thrafomond
As truly valiant as I feel him cold,
And reign'd among the choiceft of his friends,
Such as would blufh to talk fuch ferious follies,
Or back fuch bellied commendations.

King. Sir, you wrong the Prince, I gave you not
The freedom here to brave our beft of friends;
You deferve our frown.   Go to,----and be better
       temper'd.

Phil. It muft be, Sir, when I am nobler us'd.

King. Tell me what you aim at in your riddles.

Phil. Had you my eyes, Sir, and my fufferings,
My griefs upon you, and my broken fortunes,
My wants great, and now naught but hopes and
       fears,
My wrongs would make ill riddles to be laugh'd at.

2   *King.*

King. Give me your wrong in private.

Phil. Take 'em then,   [*Whispers.*
And eafe me of a load would bow ftrong Atlas.

Agr. He dares not ftand the fhock.

Cleon. I cannot blame him, there's danger in
it ; every man in this age has not a breaft of chri-
ftal for all men to read their thoughts through.
Mens hearts and faces are fo far afunder, that
they hold no intelligence. Do but view your
ftranger well, and you fhall fee a fever thro' all
his bravery. If he give not back his crown again
on the report of an elder gun, I have no augury.

King. Go to: be more of yourfelf, as you expect
Our favour, elfe you will ftir our anger ;
I muft have you know you are and fhall be at
Our pleafure : fmooth your brow, or by the gods--

Phil. I'm dead, Sir, you're my fate: it was not I
Said I was wrong'd : I carry all about me
My weak ftars lead me to; all my weak fortunes.
Who now, in all this prefence, dares (that is
A man of flefh, and is but mortal) tell me
I do not moft entirely love this Prince,
And honour his full virtues ?

King. He's poffeft.

Phil. Yes, with my father's fpirit. Tis' here O
     king !

                                        A

A dangerous fpirit, now he tells me king,
I was a king's heir, bids me be a king,
And whifpers to me thefe are all my fubjects !
'Tis ftrange he will not let me fleep, but dives
Into my fancy, and there gives me fhapes,

That kneel, and do me fervice, call me King ;
But I'll fupprefs him, 'tis a factious fpirit.

King. I do not like this ;
I'll make you tamer, or I'll difpoffefs
You both of life and fpirit : for this time
I pardon your wild fpeech, without fo much
As your imprifonment,

[*Exeunt* King, Thrafomond *and Train.*

Cleon. I thank you, Sir, you dare not for the
people.

See how his fancy labours : has he not
Spoke home and bravely ? What a dangerous train
Did he give fire to ! How he fhook the king !
Made his foul melt within him, and his blood
Run into whey ! It ftood upon his brows
Like a cold winter's dew. Let's fpeak to him,

Agr. How do you, worthy Sir ?

Phil. Well, very well ;
So well, that if it pleafe the King, I may live
Many years.

I

Cleon. The king muſt pleaſe,
Whilſt we know what you are, and who you are,
Your wrongs and merits. Shrink not, noble Sir,
But think ſtill of your father, in whoſe name
We'll waken all the gods, and conjure up
The rods of vengeance; th' abuſed people,
Who like to raging torrents ſhall ſwell high,
And ſo begirt the dens of theſe male dragons,
That thro' the ſtrongeſt ſafety they ſhall beg
For mercy at your ſword's point.

Phil. Friends, no more:
Our ears may be corrupted : 'tis an age
We dare not truſt our wills to : do you love me ?

Cleon. Do we love worth and honour ?

Phil. I thank you, Sir ;
My lord, pray is your daughter living ?

Cleon. Yes ;
And for the penance of an idle dream
Has undertaken a tedious pilgrimage.

Enter a Lady.

Phil. Is it to me you come ?

Lady. To you, brave lord.
The Princeſs would intreat your company.

Phil. The Princeſs ſend for me ? Sure you're
miſtaken.

Lady. If you are called Philander.

Phil. If she but now will love or kill me I am happy.

I will this moment attend thee to her

[*Exit with* Lady.

Cleon. Go on, and be thou as truly happy as th' art fearless.

Come, gentlemen, let us make our friends acquainted,

Left the king prove false.   [*Exeunt.*

Enter Araminta *and* Lady.

Ara. Will Philander come ?

Lady. Dear madam, you were wont to credit me at first,

Ara. But didst thou tell me he would come ?

How look'd he when he told thee he would come ?

Lady. Why, well.

Ara. And was he not a little fearful !

Lady. How ! fearful ! sure he knows not what that is.

Ara. You are all of his faction, the whole court Is bold in praise of him?

Lady. Madam, his looks methought did shew much more

Of love than fear.

Ara. Of love ! To whom ? To you ?

Lady. Madam, I mean to you.

Ara. Of love to me ! Alas ! Thy ignorance
Let's thee not fee the croffnefs of our births.
Nature that loves not to be queftioned
Why fhe did this or that, but has her ends,
And knows that fhe does well ; never gave the
- world
Two things fo oppofite, fo contrary
As he and I am.

Lady. Madam, I think I hear him.

Ara. Bring him in.
Ye gods ! that will not have your dooms withftood,
Whofe holy wifdom, at this time it is
To make the paffion of a feeble mind
The way to your great juftice. I obey.

Enter Philander.

Lady. Here is my lord Philander.

Ara. 'Tis well.----What fhall I fay ?

Phil. Madam, your meffenger
Made me believe you fent to fpeak with me.

Ara. 'Tis true, Philander, but the words are
  fuch,
So unbecoming of a virgin's mouth,

That

That I could wifh 'em faid by any other body.

Can you not guefs what 'tis that I would fay?

   Phil. When I behold

That heav'nly frame, I find fuch fweetnefs theré,

I cannot think you guilty of a thought

Which has a harfhnefs in it, much lefs a cruelty.

But then, when I confider who you are,

And what your father is, how can I chufe

But fear you muft intend my utter ruin.

   Ara. You are not well acquainted with my

      thoughts,

Tho' they are fuch as make me blufh as oft

As I would fain difcover them to you ;

Yet for my life I cannot think them ill,

Nor wifh them other, than what juft they are.

   Phil. Why won't you tell them then ?

   Ara. Becaufe I dare not tell them.

   Phil. Yes you may :

Let them be ne'er fo cruel, I will here

My doom with patience, and obey it too.

Say you would have my life, I'll give it you ;

For 'tis of me a thing fo loath'd, and of

So fmall a ufe to you, who afk it of me,

That I fhall make no price if you would have it.

                  Ara.

Ara. Why then it is your life that I muſt have,
Your whole entire life, or loſe my own.

Phil. I gladly thus reſign it to you : here,
Draw this and kill me ; I ſhall thank you for it :
For ſince my cruel fortune has decreed,
That you muſt never, madam, give conſent
To what alone can make me live with eaſe,
The dying by your hand is all I covet,

Ara. Oh ! 'tis not ſo, Philander, that I mean ;
Kill you ! no, I'd ſooner die myſelf
Than offer you but once the leaſt offence.
Why I would rather kill myſelf than live,
If 't be my fate that you would have it ſo.
By all the holy powers I would. Good gods !
Cannot you gueſs my meaning yet.

Phil. Oh heavens !
What is't ſhe means ! It cannot ſure be love ;
And yet ſhe is too full of noble thoughts
To lay a train for this contemned life,
Which ſhe might have for aſking : madam, you
Perplex my mind ſo much with what you ſay,
I know not what to think ; I know well what
To wiſh for ; I ſo earneſtly do wiſh it
That indeed I can think of nothing elſe.
'Twas not the fear of loſing of a crown

That

That gave my tongue fuch rage 'fore you this day,
The crown's a thing of which I feel no want,
But that I have it not to offer you.
There is another fear lies deeper here,
The fear of lofing that on which my life
Depends; and which I ne'er fhall tamely part with;
For, madam, know, while poor Philander lives,
'Tis but in vain your father fhall pretend
To marry you to any but----

    Ara. But to whom?

    Phil. But to him who wants the impudence to
      hope
So great a blefling: one who harbours thoughts
Of what he is fo mean and humble in
Refpect of you, that were his council afk'd
Whether or no you ought to make him happy,
He fears he hardly could advife you to it;
Who is however ftill refolved to die,
Before he fees you given to another;
And therefore on his knees begs you to kill him.

    Ara. Another foul into my body fhot,
Could not have warm'd my heart with more new
      life
Than thefe your words have done; had you but
      ftaid,
                    A little

A little longer I had vow'd the fame ;
But I am wretched now, unlefs you love me.
  Phil. Love you!
My foul adores you with fo ftrong a zeal,
So far above the rate of common love,
That mine deferves a more exalted name,
If any more exalted I could find.

  Ara. I have then no more to afk of heav'n ;
And fure our love will meet the greater blefling,
In that the greateft juftice of the gods
Is blended with it. But you mult not ftay,
Left fome unwelcome gueft fhould find you here.
Think how we may continue a fecret way
To keep intelligence betwixt us, that
On all occafions we may both agree,
Which path is beft to tread.

  Phil. I have a boy,
Sent by the gods, I think, for this intent,
Not yet feen in the court. Hunting the buck,
I found him fitting by a fountain fide,
Of which he borrow'd fome to quench his thirft,
And paid the nymph again as much in tears :
A garland by him lay, made by himfelf,
Of many feveral flowers he'd in the bay
Stuck in that myftick order, that the rarenefs

Delighted

Delighted me; but ever when he turn'd
His tender eyes upon them, he would weep,
As if he meant to make them grow again.
Seeing ſuch pretty helpleſs innocence
Dwell in his face, I aſk'd him of his ſtory.
He told me that his parents lately dy'd,
Leaving him to the mercy of the field,
Which gave him roots, and of the chriſtal ſprings,
Which did not ſtop their ſtreams; and of the ſun,
Which ſtill, he thank'd him, yielded him his light.
I gladly entertain'd him, who was as glad to follow;
And I've got the trueſt and moſt faithful boy alive,
Him will I ſend to bear our hidden love.

Enter Lady.

Lady. Madam, the Prince is come to kiſs your
  hands.

Ara. For heaven's ſake, dear Philander, hide
  yourſelf.

Phil. Hide me from Thraſomond! when thun-
  der roars,
Which is Jove's voice, tho' Jove I do revere,
I hide me not? ſhall then a foreign Prince
Have leave to brag to any foreign nation,
That he did make Philander hide himſelf?

Ara.

Ara. Why then fay nothing to him.

Phil. I'll obey.

Enter Thrafomond.

Thraf. My princely miftrefs, as true lovers ought,
I came to kifs thofe fair hands, and to fhew,
In outward ceremonies, the dear love,
Writ here within my heart.

Phil. If I can have no other anfwer,
I am gone.

Thraf. To what would he have ahfwer?

Ara. To his claim, as he pretends, to his father's crown.

Thraf. Sir, I did let you alone to-day before
the King.

Phil. Sir, do fo ftill, I would not talk with you.

Thraf. But now the time is fit. Do but name
the leaft pretence or title to a crown.

Phil. Peace, Thrafomond,—if thou——

Ara. Philander, hold.——

Phil. I have done.

Thraf. You're gone, I'll fetch you back again.

Phil. You fhall not need.

Thraf. What now?

Phil. Know, Thrafomond,

I loath

I loath to brawl with fuch a blaſt as thou,
Who art nothing but a valiant voice: but if
Thou ſhalt provoke me farther, men ſhall ſay,
Thou wert, and not lament it.

Thraſ. Do you ſlight my greatneſs ſo?
And in the chamber of the Princeſs?

Phil. It is a place, to which I muſt confeſs,
I owe a reverence. But wer't in a church,
Nay, at an altar.; there's no place ſo ſafe,
Where thou dar'ſt injure me, but.I dare kill thee;
And for your greatneſs know, Sir, I can graſp
You and your greatneſs thus, thus into nothing;
Give me not a word back.—Farewel.   [*Exit.*

Thraſ. 'Tis an odd fellow this as e'er I ſaw.
I'll ſtop his mouth hereafter with ſome office.

Ara. You had beſt to make him your counſellor.

Thraſ. I think he would diſcharge it well. But,
       Madam,
I hope our hearts are knit; but yet ſo ſlow
The ceremonies of ſtate are, that 'twill be long
Before our hands be ſo, therefore now,
Without expecting farther ceremonies,
Let us enjoy ſome ſtol'n delights together.

Ara. Since you dare utter this I muſt withdraw.
                                    [*Exit.*
                                    Thraſ.

Thraf. Nay, if you are fo fqueamifh thank
   yourfelf,
If I fhould try elfewhere.

END OF THE FIRST ACT,

A C T II,   S C E N E I.

Enter Philander; Endymion.

Phil. AND thou fhalt find her honourable, boy,
Full of regard unto thy tender youth,
For thy own modefty, and for my fake,
Apter to give than thou wilt be to afk.
   End. Sir, you did take me up when I was
      nothing;
And only yet am fomething by being yours;
You trufted me unknown; and that which you
Were apt to conftrue innocence in me,
Might have been craft; the cunning of a boy
Harden'd in lies and theft; yet ventur'd you
To part my miferies and me; for which,   -
I never can expect to ferve a lady
That bears more honour in her breaft than you.
                                        Phil.

Phil. But, boy, it will prefer thee, thou art
  young,
And bear'ſt a childiſh overflowing love
To them that ſpeak thee fair; when thy age
And judgment once ſhall end thoſe paſſions,
Thou wilt remember beſt theſe careful friends
That plac'd thee in the nobleſt way of life;
She is a Princeſs I prefer thee to.
  End. In that ſmall time that I have ſeen the
  world,
I never knew a man haſty to part
With ſervants he thought truſty : I remember
My father would prefer the boys he kept
To greater men than he; but did it not
Till they were grown too ſaucy for himſelf.
  Phil. Why, gentle boy, I find no fault at all
In thy behaviour.
  End. Sir, if I have made
A fault of ignorance, inſtruct my youth;
I ſhall be willing, if not apt to learn :
Age and experience will adorn my mind
With larger knowledge; and if I have done
A wilful fault, think me not paſt all hope
For once; what maſter holds ſo ſtrict a hand
Over his boy, that he will part with him
                                    Without

Without one warning? Let me be corrected
To break my ftubbornefs, if it be fo,
Rather than turn me off, and I fhall mend.

Phil. Thy love doth plead fo prettily to ftay,
That, truft me, I could weep to part with thee.
Alas! I do not turn thee off; thou know'ft
It is my bufinefs that doth call thee hence,
And when thou art with her, thou dwell'ft with me:
Think fo, and 'tis fo: and when time is full,
And thou haft well difcharg'd this heavy truft,
Laid on fo weak a one, I will again
With joy receive thee; as I live I will:
Nay, weep not, gentle boy, 'tis more than time
Thou did'ft attend the Princefs.

End. I am gone;
But fince I am to part with you, my lord,
And none knows whether I fhall live to do
More fervice for you, take this little pray'r;
Heav'n blefs your loves, your fights, all your de-
    figns;
May fick men, if they have your wifh, be well;
And heav'n hate thofe you curfe, tho' I be one.
                    [*Exit.*

Phil. The love of boys unto their lords is ftrange,
I have read wonders of it: yet this boy,

                              Fo

For my fake (if a man may judge by looks
And fpeech) would outdo their ftory : I may fee
A day to pay him for his loyalty.   [*Exit.*

Enter Araminta *and a* Lady.

Ara. Where is the boy?
Lady. I think within, madam.
Ara. But are his cloaths made yet?
Lady. He has 'em on.
Ara. 'Tis a pretty fad talking boy this, is
He not? I would fain know his name.
Lady. Endymion, madam.

Enter Melefinda.

Ara. Oh, you are welcome : What good news ?
Mel. As good as any one can tell your Highnefs,
That fays fhe has done that you would have wifh'd.
Ara. Haft thou difcover'd ?
Mel. Yes. I have ftrain'd a point
Of modefty for you.
Ara. I prithee how ?
Mel. In lift'ning after baudry. I perceive
Let a lady live never fo modeftly,
She will be fure to meet one time or other
Without opportunities of hearing that.

                                          Your

Your Prince, brave Thrafomond, has been fo
  amorous,
And in fo excellent a ftile !
  Ara. With whom ?
  Mel. Why, with the lady that I did fufpeĉt.
I am inform'd both of the time and place.
  Ara. O when ! and where !
  Mel. To night : her chamber.
  Ara. Run
Thyfelf into the prefence ; mingle there
With other ladies ; leave the reft to me.
If deftiny (to whom we dare not fay
Why thou didft this) have not decreed it fo,
In lafting leaves, (whofe fmalleft charaĉters
Were never alter'd) then this match fhall break.
Where is the boy ?
  Lady. Here, Madam.

Enter Endymion.

  Ara. You are fad,
I fee, to change your fervice, is't not fo ?
  End. Madam, I have not chang'd ; I wait on you
To do him fervice.
  Ara. Thou difclaim'ft me then ?
Philander told me thou canft fing and play.
                                        End.

End. If grief will give me leave, Madam, I can.
Ara. Alas, what kind of grief can thy years
  know ?
Was't a curft mafter that thou hadft at fchool ?
Thou art not capable of other grief.
Thy brows and cheeks are fmooth as waters be,
When no breath troubles them ; believe me, boy,
Care feeks out wrinkled brows and hollow eyes,
And builds himfelf caves to abide in them.
Come, Sir, pray tell me truly, does your lord
Love me ?
  End. I know not, madam, what love is:
  Ara. Can'ft thou know grief, and never yet
   knew'ft love ;
Thou art deceiv'd, boy ; does he fpeak of me
As if he wifh'd me well ?
  End. If it be love
To lofe the memory of all things elfe,
To forget all refpect of his own friends,
In thinking of your face ; if it be love
To fit crofs-arm'd, and figh away the day,
Mingled with ftarts, crying your name as loud
And haftily as men in th' ftreets do fire :
If it be love to weep himfelf away,
When he but hears of any lady dead,

   I   Or

Or kill'd, becaufe it might have been your chance;
If when he goes to reft, (which will not be)
'Twix ev'ry prayer he fays, to name you once,
As others drop a bead, be any fign
Of love, then, madam, I dare fwear he loves you.

Ara. O y' are a cunning boy, and taught to lie
For your lord's fervice: but thou know'ft a lie
That bears this found is welcomer to me,
Than any truth that fays he loves me not.
Lead the way, boy; do you attend me too;
'Tis thy lord's bufinefs haftes me thus away.

[*Exeunt.*

Enter Cleon, Agremont, Adelard, Alga, Melefinda.

Cleon. Come, ladies, fhall we talk a round? As
    men
Do walk a mile, women fhould talk an hour;
After fupper 'tis their exercife.

Mel. 'Tis late.

Alga. 'Tis all
My eyes will do to lead me to my bed. [*Exeunt.*

Enter King, Araminta, *and a guard.*

King. You gods, I fee, that who unrighteoufly
Holds wealth or ftate from others, fhall be curft

In that which meaner men are bleſt withal :
Ages to come ſhall know no male of him
Left to inherit, and his name ſhall be
Blotted from earth; if he have any child,
It ſhall be croſsly match'd: the gods themſelves
Shall ſow diviſion 'twixt her lord and her.
Yet, if it be your wills, forgive the faults
Which I have done; let not your vengeance fall
Upon this underſtanding child of mine :
She has not broke your laws; but how can I
Look to be heard of gods, who muſt be juſt,
Praying upon the ground I hold by wrong ?

Enter Cleon.

Cleon. Sir, I have aſk'd her women, but they, I
think, are bawds: I told them I muſt ſpeak with
her; they laugh'd, and ſaid their miſtreſs lay
ſpeechleſs: I ſaid my buſineſs was important;
they ſaid their lady was about it : I grew hot,
and cry'd my buſineſs was a matter that concern'd life and death ; they anſwer'd, ſo was that
which their miſtreſs was a doing. Anſwers more
direct I could not get : in ſhort, Sir, I conceive ſhe
is very well employed.

King. 'Tis then no time to dally: you o' th' guard,
Wait

Wait at the back-door of Alga's lodgings,
And fee none pafs thence upon your lives,
But bring them to me whofoe'er they be : `
Knock, gentlemen, knock louder, louder yet :
What has their pleafure ta'en away their hearing?

 Maid. Who's there that knocks fo at the dead
  of night?

 Cleon. Some friends that are come here to pay
  you a vifit.

Enter the guard, bringing in Thrafomond, *in
  drawers, muffled up in a cloak.*

 Guard. Sir, in obedience to your commands,
We ftopt this fellow ftealing out of doors.
        [*They pull off his cloak.*

 Agr. Who's this, the Prince?

 Cleon. Yes ; he's *incognito.*

 King. Sir, I muft chide you for this loofenefs :
You've wrong'd a worthy lady; but no more.

 Thraf. Sir, I came hither but to ——

 Agr. I, he's a devil at his anfwers.

 King. Conduct him to his lodgings.

Come, Sirs, break open the doors.

 Maid. You fhall not enter here.

     D 2   *Agr.*

Agr. We muft, and will.

Alga. Nay, let 'em enter; I am up and ready;
I know the bufinefs they come hither for;
'Tis the poor breaking of a lady's honour
They hunt fo after; let them have their wills.
My lord, the King, this is not noble in you,
To publifh thus the weaknefs of a woman.

King. Come down.

Alga. I dare, my lord, for all your whifpers;
This your bafe carriage fhall not ftartle me:
But I have vengeance ftill in ftore for fome,
That fhall in fpight of this your great defign,
Be joy and nourifhment to all the nation.

King. Will you come down?

Alga. I will to laugh at you.
I'll vex you to the heart, if my fkill fail not.

Cleon. 'Tis ftrange that a lady cannot ride a ftage
or two to breath herfelf, but fhe muft be ruined
for it.
If this geer holds, that lodgings be fearch'd thus,
Pray heav'n we may lye with our own wives quietly.

Enter Alga.

King. Good madam Alga, where's your honour
    now?

♪   N♦

No man can fit your palate but the Prince :
Thou moft ill-fhrouded rottennefs, thou piece
Made by a painter and apothecary.
Had'ft thou none to allure unto thy luft,
But he that muft be wedded to my daughter ?
By all the gods, all thefe, and all the pages
Shall hoot you thro' the court ; what, do you laugh ?
 Alga. Faith, Sir, your Majefty muft pardon me,
I cannot chufe but laugh to fee you merry.
If you do this, O King, or dare to think on't,
By all thofe gods you fwore by, and as many
More of my own, I will have fellows with me,
Such fellows as fhall make you noble mirth :
The Princefs, your dear daughter, fhall ftand
  by me,   ,
She fhall be hooted at as well as I.
Urge me no farther, Sir, I know her haunts,
Her layes and leaps, and will difcover all ;
Nay, will difhonour her : I know the boy
She keeps ; a handfome boy about eighteen ;
Can tell what fhe does with him ; where and when.
Come, Sir, you put me to a woman's madnefs,
The glory of a fury ; and if I
Don't do it to the height—
 King. What boy is this ?
    D 3   *Alga.*

Alga. Good-minded Prince, alas Sir, you know
        nothing;
I'm loth to utter more. Keep in this fault,
As you would keep your health, from the hot air
Of the corrupted people ; or by heav'n
I will not fall alone : what I have known
Shall be as public as a print ; nay, as
Your counfels, and by all as freely laugh'd at,

King. Has fhe a boy ?

Agr. I think I've feen one, Sir,
That waits upon her.

King. Get you to your quarter ;
For this time I will ftudy to forget you.

Alga. Do you ftudy to forget me, and I'll ftudy
        to forget you.

                    [*Exeunt* King, Alga *and guard.*

Agr. Why here's a male fpirit for Hercules ! If
ever there be nine worthies of women this wench
fhall ride aftride, and be their captain.

Cleon. Sure fhe has a garrifon of devils in her
tongue ; fhe utter'd fuch balls of wild-fire, that all
the doctors in the country will fcarce cure him :
that boy was a ftrange found-out antidote to cure
her infection. That boy, that Princefs's boy,
that brave, chafte, virtuous lady's boy, and a fair
                                        boy,

boy, a well-fpoken boy: all thefe confidered can make nothing elfe

--------- But there I'll leave you, gentlemen.

Adel. Nay, we'll go wander with you.

[*Exeunt.*

END OF THE SECOND ACT.

ACT III.   SCENE I.

Enter Cleon, Agremont, Adelard.

Agr. NAY, doubtlefs, it is true.

Cleon. I and the gods
Have rais'd this punifhment to fcourge the King
With his own iffue : is it not a fhame
For us that fhould be freemen to behold
A man that is the bravery of his age,
Philander, preft down from his royal right
By this regardlefs King? and only look
And fee the fcepter ready to be caft
Into the hands of that lacivious lady,
That lives in luft with a fmooth boy, now to be
Marry'd to yon ftrange prince, who, but that people
· Pleafe

Pleafe to let him be a Prince, is born a flave
In that which fhould be his moft noble part,
His mind.

Adel. That man that will not ftir with you
To aid Philander, let the gods forget
That fuch a creature walks upon the earth.

Agr. Philander is too backward in't himfelf ;
The gentry all wait for him, and the people,
Againft their nature long to be in arms ;
And like a field of ftanding corn that moves
With a ftiff gale, their heads bow all one way.

Cleon. The only caufe that draws Philander back
From this attempt is the fair Princefs whom
I fear he loves.

Adel. He'll not believe it then,

Cleon. Why, gentlemen, 'tis without queftion fo,

Agr. 'Tis moft true, fhe lives difhoneftly :
But how fhall we, if he be doubtful, work
Upon his faith.

Adel. Every one knows 'tis true.

Cleon. Since 'tis fo, and tends to his own good,
I'll make this new report to be my knowledge.
I'll fay I knew it; nay, I'll fwear I faw it.

Agr. It will be beft.

Adel. Yes fure, it muft needs move him.

                                        Cleon.

Cleon. Nothing but this will force him into action,

Enter Philander,

See, here he comes. Good-morrow to your grace;
We have been waiting for you.

Phil.'Worthy friends,
You that can keep your memories to know
Your friends in miseries, and cannot frown
On men disgraced for virtue; a good day
Attend you all: what service may I do
Worthy your expectation?

Cleon. My good lord,
We come to urge that virtue (which we know
Lives in your breast) forth; rise, and make head;
The nobles and the people are all dull'd
With this usurping King; and not a man
That ever heard or knew of such a thing
As virtue; but will second your attempts.

Phil. How honourable is this love in you
To me that have deserved none? Know, my friends,
(You that were born to shame your poor Philander
With too much kindness) know I could afford
To melt myself in thanks; but my designs
Are not yet ripe: let it suffice, e're long
I shall employ you; but the time's not come.

Cleon. The time is fitter some than you expect;
That

That which hereafter hardly will be reach'd
By violence, may now be caught with eafe.
As for the King, you know the people long.
Did hate him; but the Princefs now————

 Phil. Why, what
Of her, I pray?

 Cleon. Is loath'd as much as he.

 Phil. By what ftrange means?

 Cleon. She's known a whore.

 Phil. Thou ly'ft. [*Offers to draw; is held.*
And thou fhalt feel thou doft; I thought thy mind
Was full of honour; thus to rob a lady
Of her good name is an infectious fin
Not to be pardon'd; be it falfe as hell,
'Twill never be redeem'd if it be fown
Among the people, fruitful to increafe
All evil they fhall hear. Let me alone,
That I may cut off falfehood while it fprings;
Set hills on hills betwixt me and the man
That utters this, and I will fcale them all,
And from the utmoft top fall on his neck
Like thunder from a cloud.

 Cleon. This is moft ftrange.
Sir, though you love her————

 Phil. No, Sir, I love truth;

            She

She is my miſtreſs ; and who injures her
Draws vengeance from me: Sirs, let go my arms,

Adel. Nay, good my lord, be patient.

Agr. Sir, remember
Thiſi s your honour'd frieud, the good lord Cleon,
That comes to do you ſervice, and will ſhew
You why he utter'd this.

Phil. I aſk your pardon;
My zeal to truth made me unmannerly ;
Should I have heard diſhonour ſpoke of you
Behind your back, uutruly, I had been
As much diſtemper'd and enrag'd as now.

Cleon. But this is true.

Phil. O, good Sir, ſay not ſo,
Is it then true all woman-kind is falſe,
Urge it no more ; it is impoſſible :
Why ſhould you think the Princeſs could be light ?

Cleon. Becauſe, Sir, ſhe was taken in the faɛt.

Phil. 'Tis falſe; O heav'n ! 'tis falſe: it cannot be;
Can it? ſpeak, gentlemen, for the love of truth;
Is't poſſible all women ſhould be damn'd ?

Cleon. Why no, my lord.

Phil. Why, then it cannot be.

Cleon. And ſhe was taken with her boy.

Phil. What boy ?

Cleon,

Cleon. A page; a boy that ſerves her.

Phil. Oh, good gods !

A little boy.

Cleon. Ay ; know you him, my lord ?

Phil. Sin and hell; know him ! 'Sir, you are
deceiv'd :

I'll reaſon it a little coldly with you:

If ſhe were luſtful, would ſhe take a boy

That knows not yet deſire ? She would have one

Should meet her thoughts, and know the ſin he aĉts,

Which is the great delight of wickedneſs;

You are abus'd, and ſo is ſhe and I.

Cleon. How you, my lord ?

Phil. Why, all the world's abus'd

Is an unjuſt report.

Cleon. Your virtues, Sir,

Cannot look thro' the ſubtle thoughts of woman:

In ſhort, my lord, I took 'em ; I, myſelf.

Phil. Now all the devils, thou did'ſt ! Fly from
my rage ;

Would thou had'ſt taken fiends ingend'ring plagues,

When thou didſt take 'em ; hide thee from my eyes ;

Would thou had'ſt taken thunder on thy breaſt

When thou did'ſt take them, or been ſtrucken dumb

That ſo this deed for ever might have ſlept

In ſilence.   *Adel.*

Adel. Have you known him fo ill temper'd ?

Agr. Never before.

Phil. The winds that are fet loofe
From the four feveral corners of the world,
And fpread themfelves all over fea and land,
Kifs not a chafte one. What friend bears a fword
To run me through.

C'eon. Why are you mov'd at this?

Phil. When any falls from virtue I am mad ;
I am diftracted ; I've an intereft in't.

Cleon. But, good my lord, recal yourfelf, and
think
What's to be done?

Phil. I thank you : I will do't.
Pleafe you to leave me, I'll confider on't :
To-morrow I'll give you all my anfwer.

Cleon. The gods direct you.

[*Ex.* Cleon, Adel. Agr.

Phil. I had forgot to afk him where he took 'em ;
I'll follow him. O that I had a fea
Within my breaft, to quench the fire I feel :
More circumftances will but fan this fire ;
It more afflicts me now to know by whom
This deed is done, than fimply that 'tis done:
And he that tells me this is honourable,

As

As far from lies, as she is far from truth.
O that, like beasts we could not grieve ourselves
With that we see not! bulls and rams will fight
To keep their females standing in their sight;
But take them from 'em, and you take at once
Their spleens away, and they will fall again
Unto their pastures, growing fresh and fat,
And taste the waters of the springs as sweet
As 'twas before, finding no start in sleep; ·
But miserable man.----See, see, ye gods!

Enter Endymion.

He walks still, and the face you let him wear
When he was innocent, is still the same!
Not blasted! is this justice! do you mean
T' intrap mortality, that you allow
Treason so smooth a brow? I cannot now
Think he is guilty.
  End. Health to you, my Lord:
The Princess doth commend her love, her life,
And this unto you.
  Phil. Oh, Endymion,
Now I perceive she loves me; she doth shew it
In loving thee, my boy; she has made thee brave.
  End. My lord, she has attir'd me past my wish,
                      And

And paſt my merit, fit for her attendant,
Tho' far unfit for me who do attend.

Phil. Thou art grown courtly, boy; O let all
  women,
That love black deeds, learn to diſſemble here :
Here, by this paper, ſhe does write to me,
As if her heart were mines of adamant
To all the world beſides, but unto me
A maiden ſnow, that melted with my looks.
Tell me, my boy, how doth the Princeſs uſe thee;
For I ſhall gueſs her love to me by that.

End. Scarce like her ſervant, but as if I were
Something ally'd to her, or had preſerv'd
Her fame or life, with hazard of my own;
As mothers fond do uſe their only ſons ;
As I'd uſe one that's left unto my truſt,
For whom my life ſhould pay if he met harm.

Phil. Why, this is wondrous well, Endymion; but
What language pr'ythee, doth ſhe feed thee with?

End. Why, ſhe doth tell me, ſhe will truſt my
  youth
With all her loving ſecrets, and does call me
Her pretty ſervant; bids me weep no more
For leaving you, ſhe'll ſee my ſervices
Rewarded; and ſuch words, of that ſoft ſtrain,
                                        That

That I am nearer weeping when she ends,
Than e'er she does begin.
 Phil. So, so ! This is
Much better still.
  End. Are not you well, my lord.
  Phil. Well! yes, Endymion.
  End. Methinks your words
Fall not from off your tongue so evenly,
Nor is there in your looks that quietness
That I was wont to see.
  Phil. Thou art deceiv'd,
My boy. And she does stroke thy head ?
  End. Why, yes.
  Phil. And she does kiss thee ? Ha ?
  End. How's that, my lord?
  Phil. She kisses thee, my boy.
  End. Not so, my lord.
  Phil. Come, come, I know she doth.
  End. No, by my life.
  Phil. Why, then she does not love me; come
   she does,
I bad her do it; I charg'd her by all charms
Of love between us, by the hope of peace
We should enjoy, to yield thee all delights,
Naked, as to her bed : I took her oath

       Thou

Thou fhould'ft enjoy her : tell me, boy, is fhe
Not far above compare ? Is not her breath
Sweet as Arabian winds, when fruits are ripe ?
Are not her breafts two liquid ivory balls ?
Is not fhe all a lafting mine of joy ?

End. Ay, now I fee why my difturbed thoughts
Were fo perplex'd ; when firft I went to her
My heart held augury : you are abus'd,
Some villain has abus'd you : I do fee
Whereto you tend : fall rocks upon his head
That put this in you ; 'tis fome fubtle train
To bring that noble frame of yours to nought.

Phil. Thou think'ft I will be angery with thee;
  come,   '
Thou fhalt know all my drift ; I hate her more
Than I love happinefs, and plac'd thee there
To pry with narrow eyes into her deeds.
Haft thou difcover'd ? Has fhe fallen to luft,
As I would wifh her ? Speak fome comfort to me.

End. My lord, you did miftake the boy you fent :
Had fhe the luft of fparrows or of goats ;
Had fhe a fin that lay hid from the world,
Beyond the name of luft, I would not aid
Her bafe defires ; but what I came to know,

Vol. II.   E   As

As servant to her, I would not reveal,
To make my life last ages.

    Phil. Oh my heart!
This is a salve worse than the main disease.
Tell me thy thoughts, for I will know the least
That dwells within thee, or will rip thy heart
To know it: I will see thy thoughts as plain
As I now do thy face.

    End. Why, so you do.
She is, (for ought I know) by all the gods,
As chaste as ice ; but, were she foul as hell,
And I did know it thus ; the breath of kings,
The points of swords, tortures, nor bulls of brass,
Should draw it from me.

    Phil. Then it is not time
To dally with thee ; I will take thy life,
For I do hate thee ; I could curse thee now.

    End. If you do hate me, you can't curse me
          worse ;
The gods have not a punishment in store
Greater for me, my lord, than is your hate.

    Phil. Fie, fie, so young, and so dissembling too!
Tell me both when and where thou didst enjoy her,
Or plagues fall on thee if I kill thee not.

    End. Heav'n knows I never did: and when I lie

  2   To

To fave my life, may I live long and loath'd.
Hew me afunder, and I'll love the limbs,
Which you cut off, better than thefe that grow;
And kifs them dead, becaufe you made 'em fo.

   Phil. Fear'ft thou not death? Can boys con-
      temn that?

   End. Oh

What boy is he, can be content to live
To be a man that fees the very beft
Of men thus paffionate, thus without reafon?

   Phil. Oh, but thou doft not know what 'tis to die.

   End. Yes, but I do, my lord, I know it well!
'Tis lefs than to be born; a lafting fleep,
A quiet refting from all jealoufy,
A thing we all purfue : I know befides,
'Tis but the giving up a game which muft be loft.

   Phil. But there are pains, falfe boy, for perjur'd
      fouls ;
Think but on them, and then thy heart will melt.

   End. May they fall all upon me whil'ft I live,
If I be perjur'd, or have ever thought
Of that you charge me with ; if I be falfe,
Send me to fuffer in thofe punifhments
You fpeak of ; kill me.

   Phil. Oh, what fhould I do ?

                Why,

Why, who can but believe him ? He does
Swear fo earneftly, if it were not true,
The gods would not endure him. Rife, Endymion,
Thy proteftations are fo deep, and thou
Doft look fo truly when thou utter'ft them,
That, tho' I know 'em falfe as were my hopes,
I cannot urge the farther: but thou wert
To blame to injure me; for I muft love
Thy honeft looks, and never take revenge
Upon thy tender youth: a love from me to thee
Is firm, whate'er thou doft.. It troubles me
That I have call'd the blood out of thy cheeks,
That did fo well become them ; but, good boy,
Let me not fee thee more ; fomething is done
That will diftract me ; that will raife a ftorm
Within my breaft too great for me to quell,
If thou com'ft near me..

    End. I will fly as far
As there is morning, e'er I give diftafte
To that moft honour'd mind. But thro' thefe tears,
Shed at my hopelefs parting, I can fee
A world of treafon practis'd upon you,
And her and me.   Farewel for evermore ;
If you fhall here that forrow ftruck me dead,
And after find me loyal, let there be

                      A tear,

A tear, at leaft, fhed by you for me; and
I then fhall reft in peace. *[Exit.*

Phil. Bleffings be with thee,
Whatever thou deferv'ft. O where fhall I
Go bath this body? Nature too unkind,
That made no med'cine for a troubled mind. *[Exit.*

Enter Araminta.

Ara. I marvel my boy comes not back again;
But that I know my love will queftion him
Over and over, how I flept, wak'd, talk'd;
How often his dear name was mention'd by me;
How I figh'd, wept, and fung, and thoufand more
Such things? I fhould be angry at his ftay.

Enter King.

King. What, at your meditations? Who is with
you?

Ara. None but my fingle felf; I need no guard:
I do no wrong, nor fear none.

King. Have you not a boy?

Ara. Yes, Sir.

King. What kind of boy?

Ara. A waiting boy.

King. A handfome boy?

E 3

Ara.

Ara. A very handfome boy.

King. He talks and fings, and plays?

Ara. I think he does.

King. About eighteen?

Ara. I never afk'd his age.

King. Pray, is he full of fervice?

Ara. Why do you afk!

King. Put him away.

Ara. How, Sir!

King. Put him away.

'Has done you that good fervice, I'm afham'd
To fpeak of.

Ara. Good Sir, let me underftand you.

King. If you fear me, fhew it in duty; put
Away that boy.

Ara. Let me have reafon for it,
And then' your will to me fhall be a law.

King. Do you not blufh to afk it? Caft him off,
Or I fhall do the fame to you: Y' are one
Shame with me, and fo near unto myfelf,
That, by my life, I dare fcarce tell myfelf
What you have done.

Ara. What have I done, my lord?

King. It is a language that all love to learn;
The common people fpeak it well already:

They

They need no grammar; underftand me well,
There be foul whifpers ftirring; caft him off,
And fuddenly, I charge you do't. Farewel. [*Exit.*

Ara. Where may a maiden live fecurely free,
Keeping her honour fafe ? Not with the living;
They feed upon the opiniohs, errors, dreams,
And make 'em truths: they draw a nourifhment
Out of defaming, grow upon difgraces,
And when they fee a virtue fortify'd
Strongly, above the batt'ry of their tongues,
Oh, how they caft about to ruin it !

Enter Philander.

Phil. Peace be to your fair thoughts, my deareft
    miftrefs.

Ara. O dear Philander, I've a war within me.

Phil. He muft be more than man that makes
    thefe chryftals
Run into rivers: fweeteft fair; the caufe ?
And, as I am your flave, ty'd to your goodnefs,
Your creature made again from what I was,
And newly fpirited: I'll right your honour.

Ara. Oh, my beft love, that pretty boy------

Phil. What boy ?

Ara. The pretty boy you gave me.

Phil. What of him ?

Ara.

Ara. Muft be no more mine.

Phil. Why?

Ara. They're jealous of him.

Phil. Who's jealous?

Ara. The King is.

Phil. Oh my fortune!

Then 'tis no idle ftory.   Let him go.

Ara. O cruel! what! are you hard-hearted too?
Who now fhall bring you word how much I love
    you?
Who now fhall weep to you the tears I fend?
Who now fhall give you letters, rings and bracelets?
Wafte tedious nights in ftories of your praife?
And throw away his health in ferving you?
Who fhall take up his lute, and, finging to it,
Charm me afleep, making me dream, and cry,
Oh my dear, dear Philander?

    Phil. Oh my heart!
Would he had broken thee that made thee know
This Lady was not true. Madam, forget
This boy; I'll get you one a great deal better.

    Ara. Oh never, never fuch a boy again
As my Endymion is.

    Phil. 'Tis but your fancy.

    Ara. With thee, my boy, farewel for evermore

I   All

All fecrecy in fervants; farewel faith,
And all defire to do well, for itfelf:
Let all that fhall fucceed thee, for thy wrongs,
Betray chafte love.

   Phil. And all this paffion for
A boy?

   Ara. He was your boy; you put him to me:
The lofs of fuch a one requires a mourning.

   Phil. Oh, thou forgetful woman!

   Ara. How, my lord?

   Phil. Falfe Araminta; thou haft quite undone
     me.

Haft thou a med'cine to reftore my wits
Again, when I have loft 'em? Oh ye gods!
Give me a worthy patience: have I ftood
Alone the fhock of all the worft misfortunes?
Have I feen mifchiefs numberlefs and mighty
Grow like a fea upon me? Have I taken
Dangers as ftern as death into my bofom,
And laugh'd upon 'em, made them but a mirth,
And flung 'em off? Do I live under this
Ufurping King, like one, who languifhing
Hears his fad bell, and fees his mourners by?
Do I bear all this bravely, and muft fink
At length under a woman's falfhood? O
                         That

That boy, that curs'd boy! None but a boy
To eafe your luft?

Ara. Why, did he tell you fo?

Phil. It may be, he did.

Ara. Alas, then I'm undone.
I fee the plot caft for my overthrow.

Phil. Now you may take that little right I have
To this poor kingdom; give it to your joy,
For I have no joy in it. Some far place
Where never womankind durft fet her foot,
I'll feek to curfe you in.

Ara. Oh, I am wretched!

Phil. There dig a cave, and preach to birds
   and beafts,
What woman is, and help to fave 'em from you;
How heav'n is in your eyes; but in your hearts
More hell than hell has: how your tongues like
   fcorpions,
Both heal and poifon; how your thoughts are
   woven
With thoufand changes in one fubtle web,
And woven fo by you: how that foolifh man
That reads the ftory of a woman's face,
And dies believing it, is loft for ever.
How all the good you have is but a fhadow;

                                             I' th'

I' th' morning with you, and at night behind you,
Paſt and forgotten. How your vows are froſts,
Faſt for a night, and with the next ſun gone.
How you are, being taken all together,
A meer confuſion, and ſo dead a chaos,
Truth's love can diſtinguiſh nothing in you. Theſe
Sad texts till my laſt hour I am bound to utter.
So farewel all my woe, all my delight.   [*Exit.*

Ara Be merciful, ye gods, and ſtrike me dead;
What way have I deſerved this? Make my breaſt
Tranſparent as pure cryſtal, that the world,
Jealous of me, may ſee the fouleſt thought
My heart does hold. Where ſhall a woman turn
Her eyes to find out conſtancy? Save me!

Enter Endymion,

How black, methinks, that guilty boy looks now!
O thou diſſembler! that before thou ſpak'ſt
Wert't in thy cradle falſe! ſent to make lies
And betray innocents! thy lord and thou
May glory in the aſhes of a maid
Fool'd by her paſſion, but the conqueſt is
Nothing ſo great as wicked. Fly away,
Let my command force thee to that, which ſhame
Should do without it. If thou underſtood'ſt
                                        The

The loath'd office thou haft undergone,
Why, thou would'ft hide thee under heaps of hills,
Left men fhould dig, and find thee.

    End. Oh, what god,
Angry with men, hath fent this ftrange difeafe
Into the nobleft minds? Madam, this grief
You add unto me, is no more than drops
To feas, for which they are not feen to fwell:
My lord has ftruck his anger through my heart,
And let out all the hopes of future joys.
You need not bid me fly; I came to part,
To take my lateft leave: farewel for ever.
I durft not run away, in honefty,
From fuch a lady, like a boy that ftole,
Or made fome grievous fault; the pow'r of gods
Affift you in your fufferings; hafty time
Reveal the truth to your abus'd lord,
And mine: that he may know your worth, whilft I
Go feek out fome forgotten place to die.   [*Exit.*

    Ara. Peace guide thee, thou haft overthrown me
      once,
Yet if I had another Troy to lofe,
Thou or another villain, with thy looks,
Might talk me out of it, and fend me with
My hair difhevel'd, through the fiery ftreets.

                Enter

Enter a Lady.

Lady. Madam, the King has fent for you in
.hafte,
To go abroad with him.
Ara. Whither, d'ye know ?
Lady. A hunting, madam.
Ara. I'm in tune to hunt.
Diana, if thou can'ft rage with a maid,
As with a man, let me difcover thee
Bathing, and turn me to a fearful hind,
That I may die, purfued by cruel hounds,
And have my ftory written in my wounds.

[*Exeunt.*

END OF THE THIRD ACT.

A C T   IV.   S C E N E   I.

Enter Philander.

Phil. **O**H .that I had been nourifhed in thefe
woods
With milk of goats and acorns, and not known
The right of crowns, nor the diffembling trains
Of

Of womens looks ; but dig'd myfelf a cave,
Where I may fire, my cattle and my fhed
Might have been fhut together in one bed ;
And then have taken me fome mountain girl,
Beaten with winds, chafte as the harden'd rocks
Whereon fhe dwells ; that might have ftrew'd my
    bed
With leaves and reeds, and with the fkins of
    beafts,
And born at her big breafts my large courfe iffue.
This had been a life free from vexation.

Enter Endymion.

End. Oh wicked men ! an innocent may walk
Safe among beafts ; nothing affaults me here.
See ! there my troubled lord fits, as his foul
Were fearching out a way to leave his body.
It grieves me that I'm forc'd to difobey
His laft commands ; but 'tis not in my pow'r
To forbear fpeaking, when I look on him.
I'll make as if I wanted, tho' heav'n knows
I can't, becaufe I do not wifh to live.
You that are griev'd can pity ; hear my lord.

Phil. Is there a creature yet fo miferable
That I can pity ?

                                End.

End. Oh, my noble lord,
View my ſtronge fortune, and beſtow on me
Out of good nature (if my ſervices
Can merit nothing) ſo much as may help
To keep this little piece I hold of life
From cold and hunger.

    Phil. Is it thou ? Go ſell,
For ſhame, thoſe miſbecoming cloaths thou wear'ſt,
And feed thyſelf with them.

    End. Alas, my lord,
I can get nothing for them ; people here
Think it were treaſon for them but to touch
Such gay, fine things.

    Phil. Now, by my life, this is
Unkindly done to vex me with thy ſight ;.
Thou'rt fallen back to thy diſſembling trade.
How ſhould'ſt thou think to cozen me again ?
Remains there yet a plague untry'd for me ?
Ev'n ſo thou wept'ſt when firſt I took thee up ;
Wretch that I was to do ſo ; if thy tears
Can work on any other, uſe thy art,
I'll not betray it. Which way wilt thou take,
That I may ſhun thee ? for thy eyes to mine
Are poiſon ; and I'm loth to grow in rage :
Say, which way wilt thou take ?

                                      End.

End. Which way you pleafe :
Since I can't go with you.   I have no choice;
But I'm refolv'd where'er I go to have
That path in chafe which leads unto my grave.

[*Exeunt feverally.*

Enter Cleon, *and the* Woodmen.

Cleon. This is the ftrangeft fudden change! You
Woodmen.

1 *Wood.* My lord Cleon.

Cleon. Saw you a lady come this way on a fable
horfe, and ftubb'd with ftars of white?

2 *Wood.* Was fhe not young and tall?

Cleon. Yes. Rode fhe to the wood or to the plain?

3 *Wood.* Faith, my lord, we faw none.

[*Ex. Woodmen.*

Enter Agremont.

Cleon. Pox o' your queftions then.   What is fhe
found?

Agr. Nor will be, I think.

Cleon. Let him feek his daughter himfelf? fhe
cannot ftir about a little neceffary bufinefs, but
the whole court muft be in arms; when fhe has
done, we fhall have peace.

Agr.

Agr. There's already a thoufand fatherlefs tales amongſt us; fome fay her horfe run away from her; fome a wolf purfu'd her! others it was a plot to kill her; and that arm'd men were feen in the wood; but queſtionlefs fhe rode away willingly.

Enter King *and* Adelard.

King. Where is fhe?

Agr. Sir, I cannot tell.

King. How's that?
If thou doſt anfwer fo——

Agr. Sir, fhall I lie?

King. Yes; and be damn'd, rather than tell me
  that;
I fay again, where is fhe? Mutter not;
Sir, fpeak you where fhe is.

Cleon. I do not know.

King. Speak that again fo boldly, and by heav'n
It is thy laſt; you, fellows, anfwer me;
Where is fhe? mark me all, I am your King;
I wiſh to fee my daughter, fhew me her,
I do command you all, as you are fubjeĉts,
To fhew her me; what am I not your King?
And are you not t' obey what I command.

Cleon. Yes; if the thing be poſſible and honeſt.

King. Be poffible and honeft? Hear me, thou,
Thou traytor, that confin'ft thy King to what
Is poffible and honeft ; fhew her me.

    Cleon. Indeeed I can't, till I know where fhe is.

    King. You have betray'd me ; you have loft my
      life,
The jewel of my life ; go, bring her me,
And fet her here before me; 'tis the King
Will have it fo ; whofe breath can ftill the winds,
Uncloud the fun, charm down the fwelling feas,
And ftop the floods of heav'n : can't it ! Speak.

    Cleon. No.

    King. No? Cannot the breath of Kings do this?

    Cleon. No; nor fmell fweet itfelf, if once the
      lungs
Be but corrupted.

    King. Is it fo ? Take heed.

    Cleon. Sir, take you heed you do not dare the
      pow'rs
That muft be juft.

    King. Alas, what are we Kings ?
Why do you, gods, place us above the reft
To be ferv'd, flatter'd, and ador'd, till we
Believe we hold within our hands your thunder ;
And when we come to try the pow'r we have,

                           There's

There's not a single leaf shakes at our threatning?
I've sinn'd, 'tis true, and here stand to be punish'd;
Yet would not thus be punish'd: let me chuse
My way, and lay it on.

Cleon. He articles with heav'n; would somebody
would draw the bonds for the performance of co-
venants betwixt them.

Enter Thrasomond, Melesinda, *and* Alga.

King. What, is she found?

Thras. No; we have ta'en her horse,
He gallop'd empty by.

King. You, Melesinda, rode with her into
The wood: why left you her?

Mel. She bid me do't.

King. What if she did? You should not have
  obey'd.

Mel. 'Twould ill become my fortunes and my
  birth
To disobey the daughter of my King.

King. Y'are willing to obey us for our hurt;
But I will have her.

Thras. If I have her not,
There shall be no more Sicily by heav'n.

       Cleon.

Cleon. Why, what will he carry it away in's pocket?

King. I fee the injuries I've done muft be
Reveng'd.

Cleon. But this will never find her out.

King. Run all; difperfe yourfelves; whoe'er
    he be,
That can but bring her to me, fhall be happy.

Thraf. Come, let us feek.

Cleon. Each man a feveral way.   [*Exeunt.*

Enter a Country Fellow.

Clown. I'll fee the king if he be in the foreft; I
have hunted him thefe two hours; if I fhould go
home, and not fee him, my fifter would laugh at
me. I can meet with nothing but people better
hors'd than myfelf, that out-ride me; nor can I
hear any thing but fhouting: thefe Kings had
need of good brains? this whooping is able to
put a mean man out of his wit. Well, I'll about
it again.   [*Exit.*

Enter Araminta.

Ara. Where am I now? Feet, find me out a way,
Without the counfel of my troubled head;

I'll

I'll truſt you boldly amidſt all theſe woods;
O'er mountains, through brambles, pits, and
  floods.
Heav'n I hope will eaſe me: I am ſick.

Enter Endymion.

End. Yonder's my honour'd lady, faſt aſleep:
I fear ſhe faints; the lovely red is gone
To guard her heart: ſhe breaths not.   Madam,
Open once more thoſe roſy twins, and ſend
To my dear lord your laſt farewel.   She ſtirs.
How is it, madam, pray?
    Ara. 'Tis not well done
To put me in a miſerable life,
And hold me there: I pray thee let me go;
I ſhall do beſt without thee: I am well,

Enter Philander.

Phil. I was to blame to be ſo much in rage;
I'll tell her truly when and where I heard
This killing truth; I will be temperate
In ſpeaking, and as juſt in hearing too.
Oh monſtrous! Tempt me not, ye gods; good gods,
Tempt not a frail man: what's he that has a heart,
But he muſt eaſe it here?
            F 3   *End.*

End. Are you not better yet ?

Ara. I'm well, forbear.

Phil. Let me love lightning, let me be embrac'd
And kifs'd by vipers rather than bear this.
Defpair dwell with you; what before my face ?
Nature invent a curfe, and throw it on you :
May poifon grow between your lips, difeafes
Be your brood : I'll part you once at leaft.

　　　　　[*Runs at* Endymion, *and hurts* Araminta.

Ara. Oh, dear Philander, leave to be inrag'd,
And hear me.

Phil. I have done ; not the calm fea, .
When Æolus locks up his windy crew,
Is lefs difturb'd than I: thus you fhall know it;
Dear Araminta, do but take this fword,
And feel how temperate a heart I have ;
Then you, and this your boy, may live and reign
In luft, without controul. Wilt thou, Endymion ?
I pri'thee kill me : thou art poor, and may'ft
Nourifh ambitious thoughts ; were I but dead
There would be nothing then to hinder thee.
Am I mad now ? Pray fpeak : I'm fure I were,
If after all the wrongs I have receiv'd,
I fhould defire to live : you will not kill
Me then ?

　　　　　　　　　　　　End.

End. Not for a world.

Phil. I blame not thee,
Thou haft done but that
Which gods would have
Transform'd themfelves to do. Be gone ;
Leave me without reply. This is the laft [*Exit End.*
Of all our meetings : come then, kill me with
This fword; be wife, left worfe might follow ; one
Of us muft die.

Ara. Indeed I think I muft ;
My wound begins to make me faint already.

Phil. How ? What wound ? Where ?

Ara. O, touch me gently, there :
I hope 'twill give me eafe in t' other world,
For I could never yet find any here.

Phil. My cruel ftars, what have you brought
  upon me !
Now I defy you all to do your worft.

Ara. But tell me, pray, are there no jealoufies,
No flanders, where I'm going ? No ill there ?

Phil. O, fay no more, but help to ftop thy wound ;
It was not meant to thee, but to the boy ;
That vile ungrateful boy.

Ara. Would you not then have kill'd me? Pray
  fay no,
Whate'er you meant.   *Phil.*

Phil. Can I hear this, and live ?
Why would you make me mad? Force me to do
I know not what, and hurt you? Why would you
Difgrace me thus ? Why did you love the boy?
(Curfe on th' unhappy hour when I was born !)
How could you find i' your heart to ufe me fo?

Ara. Alas, my foul doats only upon you,
And çan love nothing elfe, whate'er you do.

Enter Clown.

Clown. Hey day ! What have we here ?
Phil. Ha ! ha ! What art thou ?
Clown. A courtier with his naked fword upon a
woman ! I think the rogue has hurt her too ; I'm
fure fhe bleeds. By'r leave, fair lady, who has
hurt you fo ?
Phil. Good honeft friend, purfue thy own affairs.
Clown. Friend me no friends ; I'll know who
hurt the woman.
Phil. Nay leave us firrah, or thou fhalt repent it.
Clown. Say'ft thou fo, boy, I will try that i'faith.
Phil. Slave, doft thou dare me thus ?
[*They fight.*]
Ara. Heav'ns guard my lord.

[*Clown*

[*Clown falls.*]

Phil. The gods take part againſt me ſure, this
    boor

[*Noiſe within.*]

Could ne'e have hurt me elſe. Here's people
    coming.

What ſhall I do ? Alas what ſhall I think ?

I heard her pray for me when I was fighting,

Perhaps ſhe may be injur'd. O my fate !

I either am diſhonour'd, or a wretch

To be deſpis'd ; the very worſt of men.

[*Noiſe again*]

Ara. Fly, fly, my lord, or your dear life is loſt.

Phil. D' ye think I'll leave you thus to ſave my
    life ?

Ara. Do it then pray, Philander, to ſave mine ;

For if you ſtay indeed I'll bleed to death ;

It is not hard to do : and yet methinks

My wound is nothing now y' are ſorry for't.

As ſoon as you are ſafe I ſhall be well.

Phil. But I muſt never hope to be ſo more.

Kill me, and pardon me ; 'tis all I beg.

Farewel then ; if thou'rt true, I'll kill myſelf ;

And tho' thou ſhould'ſt deſerve the worſt of
    thoughts,

                        However,

However, I forgive thee all thy faults.   [*Exit.*

Enter Thrasomond, Cleon, Agremont, Adelard,
    and Woodmen.

Thras. What art thou?

Clown. Almost kill'd I am for a foolish woman;
a knave has hurt her.

Thras. The Princess, gentlemen! Where's the
    wound, madam?
Is it dangerous?

Ara. He has not hurt me.

Clown. I say she lyes; he has hurt her in the side;
Look else.

Thras. O sacred spring of innocent blood!

Cleon. 'Tis above wonder who should do this.

Ara. I feel it not.

Thras. Speak, villain; who has hurt the Princess?

Clown. Is it the Princess?

Cleon. I.

Clown. Then I have seen something yet.

Thras. But who has hurt her?

Clown. I told you a rogue: I ne'er saw him before.

Thras. Madam, who did it?

Ara. Some dishonest wretch: alas I know him
not, and do forgive him.

                                        Clown.

Clown. He's hurt too, he cannot go far : I made my father's old fox fly about his ears.

Thraf. How will you have me kill him ?

Ara. Not at all ; 'tis fome diftracted fellow.

Thraf. By this hand I'll leave ne'er a piece of him bigger than a nut, and bring him all in my hat.

Ara. Nay, good Sir, if you do take him, bring
      him to me
Alive ; and I'll invent fome punifhment
For him, great as his fault.

Thraf. I will.

Ara. But fwear.

Thraf. Why then i'fecks I will. Wait you upon The Princefs : Woodmen, lead off this poor man. Come, gentlemen, let us purfue our chafe.

          [*Exeunt* Thraf. Cleon, Agr. Adel.
          [1 Wood *and* Araminta.

Clown. I pray you, friend, let me fee the King.

2 *Wood.* That you fhall, and receive thanks.

Clown. If I get clear with this, I'll go no more to gay fights in hafte.   [*Exeunt.*

Enter Endymion.

End. A heavinefs near death fits on my brow, And I muft fleep ; bear me, thou gentle bank

                            For

For ever if thou wilt; you fweet ones all,
Let me unworthy prefs you ; I could wifh,
I rather were a coarfe ftrew'd o'er with you
Than quick above you ; dulnefs fhuts my eyes,
And I am giddy: O, that I could take
So found a fleep as I might never wake,

Enter Philander.

Phil. Whether fhall I go now, or rather why
Should I go any farther ? True, I'll end
My journey here.   What fhould I travel for.
With fuch an odious, tirefome load upon me,
As now, alas, my life is grown ? And which
I muft not hope to fave whate'er falls out :
For if fhe's falfe, I'm fure I cannot live ;
And if fhe fhould prove true, I'd fcorn to do't,
After the injuries I've bafely done her.
Oh why fhould we thus madly be inclin'd
To think the worfe of thofe we love the moft ?
Ye gods, is it to great a tyranny to plague
Mankind at once with love and jealoufy,
Who's this ? Endymion fleeping ! 'Tis unjuft
Thy fleep fhould be fo found, and mine whom thou
Haft wrong'd, fo broken. I hope he will not wake :
I'm very loath to kill him, but I feel

Some-

Something within me that would force me to't :
If I fhould but once more behold his eyes,
They are the caufe of all my miferies;
Yet fhe did vow to me fhe loves him not;
But who is he dares truft to woman's tongues ?
They are fo us'd to talk before they think,
They know not how to mean one word they fay.
I'm fure I faw him take her in his arms ;
And he deferves to lofe his life for that.

       [Endymion *wakes.*

 End. I cannot fleep, my heart's too full of
  grief ;
No fooner are my eye-lids clos'd, but ftraight
Methinks I fee Philander in a rage,
Ready to ftrike me dead.   Sure there he ftands :
It muft be he, for none was ever like him :
I cannot bear his hatred any longer ;
I'll fpeak, tho' he fhould kill me for't.   Can you,
My lord, be angry with me ftill ?

 Phil. Forbear ; ·
If thou com'ft near thou wilt compel me to
An act I would avoid.

 End. Pray, hear me firft.

 Phil. Begone.

 End. I can't.

          Phil.

Phil. then take what thou deserv'ft.

                    [*Wounds him.*

End. Bleft be that hand again ; for pity's fake.

Phil. My legs now fail me quite with lofs of
    blood ;

Take your revenge ; I'll teach you cruelty :

It was this lucklefs hand that hurt the Princefs.

Tell my purfuers, you received your wound

In ftaying me, and I will fecond it. [*Noife without.*

End. Oh fly, and fave yourfelf, my lord.

Phil. How's this ?

Would'ft thou I fhould be fafe ?

End. Elfe it were vain

For me to live ; the wound you gave me has

Not yet bled much ; reach me that noble hand,

I'll help to cover you.

Phil. Art thou then true ?

End. Or let me perifh loath'd ; come, my good
    lord,

Creep in among thefe bufhes ; who does know

But that the gods may fave your precious life ?

Phil. Then fhall I die for grief, if not for this,

That I have wounded thee ; what wilt thou do?

End. Shift well enough for one, I warrant you.

Within. Follow, follow ; that way they went.

                       End.

End. With my own wound I'll bloody my own
    fword,
I need not counterfeit to fall, heav'n knows,
That I can ftand no longer.

Enter Thrafamond, Cleon, Agremont, *and* Adelard.

    Thraf. I'm fure,
To this place we have tracked him by his blood.
    Ara. Yonder creeps one away.
    Cleon. Stay, what are you?
    End. A wretched creature, wounded in thefe
    woods
By beafts; relieve me, if your names be men,
Or I fhall perifh.
    Cleon. This is he, my lord,
Upon my foul, that hurt her; 'tis the boy
That ferv'd her.
    Thraf. O thou damn'd in thy creation,
What caufe had'ft thou to hurt the Princefs?
    Speak.
    End. Then I'm betray'd.
    Cleon. No, apprehended, Sir.
    End. Well, I confefs the fact, urge it no more.
I fet upon the Princefs, and defign'd
Her death: for charity, let fall at once

                      The

The punishment you mean, and do not load
This weary flesh with tortures.

 Thraf. I will know
Who hir'd thee to this.

 End. My own revenge.

 Thraf. Revenge! for what?

 End. It pleas'd her to receive
Me for her page, and when my fortunes ebb'd;
(As rivers, being unfupply'd, grow dry)
And men ftride o'er them carelefly; fhe pour'd
Her welcome graces on my wants, and fwell'd
My ftreams fo high, that they o'erflow'd their
  banks.
Threatning deftruction to who'er durft crofs 'em.
But then as fwift as ftorms rife at fea,
She cafts her firey eyes like lightning on me,
And in an inftant blafted all my hopes;
And left me worfe, and more contemned by far
Than other little brooks, becaufe I had
Been great: in fhort, I knew I could not live,
And therefore did defire to die reveng'd.

 Thraf. I'll torture ye i'fecks.

 Agr. Come lead him hence.

      [Philander *creeps out.*]

 Phil. Turn back, you raverfhers of innocence:

I

         Know

Know you the price of that you bear away
So rudely.

Adel. Who is this?

Cleon. The lord Philander.

Phil. 'Tis not the treafure of all Kings in óne,
The wealth of Tagus, nor thé rocks of pearl
That pave the court of Neptune, can weigh down
This virtue: it was I that hurt the Princefs.
Place me fome god upon a pyramid,
Higher than hills of earth, and lend a voice
Loud as your thunder to me; that from thence
I may declare to all the under world
The worth that dwells in him:

    Thraf. Who's this?

    End. My lord, fome man that's weary of his life.

    Phil. Leave thefe untimely courtefies, Endymion.

    End. Alas; he's mad; come will you lead me on?

    Phil. By all the oaths that men ought moft to
      keep
And gods do punifh moft when they are broken,
He touch'd her not. Take heed, Endymion,
How thou doft drown the virtues thou haft fhewn
With perjury: by all that's good, 'twas I:
You know fhe ftood betwixt me and my right.

    Agr. It was Philander.

Cleon. It is a brave boy.

Adel. I fear,

We were all deceiv'd.

Phil. Have I no friend here ?

Cleon. Yes.

Phil. Pray fhew it then,

Somebody lend a hand to draw me near him.

Would you have tears fhed for you when you die ?

Then lay me gently on his neck, that there

I may weep floods, and breath my fpirit out.

'Tis not the wealth of Plutus, nor the gold

Lock'd in the heart of earth, can buy away

This armful from me: you hard-hearted men,

More ftony than thefe mountains, can you fee

Such pure blood drop, and not cut off your flefh

To ftop it with ? Queens ought to tear their hair

To bind thefe wounds, and bath them with their

tears.

If I had ftrength, I'd pluck my heart out.   Oh,

Endymion ! thou that art the wealth of poor

Philander, and that I have us'd fo ill ;

Pray, let my crimes be punifh'd as they ought,

And don't forgive me, I deferve it not.

Enter King, &c.

King. What, is the villain ta'en ?

Thraf.

Thraſ. Both theſe confeſs the deed.

Phil. Sir, queſtion it no more, 'twas I.

King. The fellow, that did fight with him will
    tell.

Ara. Ay me! I know he will.

King. You know him ſurē.

Ara. No Sir; if it was he, he was diſguis'd.

Phil. I was ſo.   O why am I not yet dead?

King. Thou vain, ambitious fool, thou that haſt
    laid

A train for thy own life; now I do mean .

To do; I'll leave to talk.   Bear him to priſon.

  Ara. Sir, they did plot together to take hence

This harmleſs life; ſhould it paſs unreveng'd,

I ſhould to earth go weeping; grant me then

(By all the love a father bears his child)

Their cuſtody, and that I may appoint

Their tortures, and the way they are to die.

  King, 'Tis granted; take them to you with a
    guard.

Come, princely, Thraſomond, this buſineſs paſt,

We may with more ſecurity go on

To our intended match.

           [*Exeunt all, but* Cleon *and* Agremont.

         G 2   *Agr.*

Agr. This action of Philander, I'm afraid
Will lofe the people's hearts.

Cleon. No; fear it not;
Their fubtlety will think it but a trick.

Enter Adelard.

Agr. How are his wounds?

Adel. They are but fcratches; it
Was only lofs of blood that made him faint.

Cleon. Come, let's go fee him.

Adel. No; not yet: the King
Has told the Princefs he'll be with her ftraight,
And that he will examine there Philander
About his plot, and his confederates.

Cleon. Sure if he had a plot, he'd tell us on't.
But what a devil made him hurt the Princefs,
I can't imagine what all this fhould mean.

END OF THE FOURTH ACT.

ACT

A C T V.   S C E N E I.

Philander, Araminta, Endymion.

Ara. NAY, dear Philander, pray lament no more.

End. For heav'n's fake give o'er; we're very
well.

Phil. Oh Araminta, oh Endymion, leave
To be thus kind; I fhall be fhut from heav'n,
As now from earth, if you continue fo.
I am a man that has abus'd a pair
Of the moft trufty ones earth ever bore:
Can it ftill bear us all? Forget me, pray,
Think that fo great a wretch could not be born,
As was Philander. And for thee, my boy,
I fhall declare words that will mollify
The hearts of beafts, to fpare thy innocence.

End. Alas! my lord, my life is not a thing
Worthy your noble thoughts: 'tis not a life,
'Tis but a piece of childhood thrown away.
Should I out-live you, I fhould then out-live
Virtue and honour; and when that day comes,
If ever above once I clofe thefe eyes,
May I live fpotted for my perjury.

Ara. And I the miferableft maid alive,

Da;

Do, by the honour of a virgin, vow
Never to quit you.

Phil. Make me not fo hated:
People will tear me, when they find you true
To fuch a wretch as me : I fhall die loath'd.
Enjoy your kingdom peaceably, whilft I
For ever fleep forgotten with my faults.
Every juft fervant, every maid in love
Will have a piece of me, if you be true.

End. A piece of you! he muft be one not born
Of whom, that can cut it, and look on.

Phil. Take me in tears betwixt you; for• my
    heart
Will break with fhame and forrow.

Ara. Grieve no more.

Phil. Pray tell me now; if you had wrong'd me
    bafely,
And found your life no price compar'd to mine ?
What is't you would have done ?

End. It was a miftake.

Phil. What if it were ?

End. We would have afk'd your pardon.

Phil. And hope t' enjoy it too.

Ara. Enjoy it! yes.

Phil. Would you indeed ? Be plain.

I   *End.*

End. We would, my lord.

Phil. Forgive me then.

Ara. So, fo, 'tis well.
Are all things ready for our marriage?

End. I'll go fee;
Learn all to love without defign from me. [*Exit.*

Phil. Lead to my death.

Ara. I hope not fo; at leaft
Thus much I'm fure of, that I won't out-live you;
And that I might the better claim a right
To end my days with yours, I have a prieft
Ready to join our hands and hearts together.

Phil. Can there be yet a new invention found
Still more to fhame Philander? I muft now
Fly from her love, or be her murderer.

Ara. What means this paufe? Why won't you
    fpeak to me?

Phil. I know not which is worft; O my dear
    foul,
I dare not truft your father's cruelty;
He is grown hot and fpeedy in his rag e.
And now I'm mafter of myfelf again,
It is not in my power to do you harm.

Ara. Nothing can harm me but your want of love,
I dread your coldnefs, not his heat nor rage.

G 4

Phil.

Phil. Ay, but his hatred againſt me is ſuch,
He would deſtroy you too if you were mine.

Ara. What if he did; I ſhould take pleaſure in't,
Had I but you, Philander, in my arms.

Phil. Dear Araminta, preſs me not ſo far;
Try not my paſſion with too ſtrong a teſt;
Lovers can never very long be wiſe;
They go too faſt to keep a ſteady pace,
And mind with too much violence preſent things
To take their meaſures right of what's to come:
If you inflame me more, my love will grow
So wild, I ſhall not have one cool thought left,
And then I ſhall undo thee.

Ara No, you'll make
Me bleſt; of all the race of womankind
Moſt happy.

Phil. But yet I——

Ara. What?

Phil. I'm afraid.

Ara. Do not torment me thus, if it's for love
Of me you are ſo; mark what I ſhall ſay;
For heav'n ne'er yet declared a greater truth;
Marry me ſtraight, before my father comes,
(And you forget how ſoon he will be here,)
Or, by your life, which I prize more than mine,

I'll

I'll kill myfelf.

Phil. Nay, then I muft obey:
And pardon me, my deareft Araminta,
If I, at fuch a time of joy as this,
Can yet have griefs about me: but I have,
To find that I'm outdone, tho' by thyfelf,
So far in all the kindeft proofs of love.

   Ara. Ah, could my death to the whole world
     proclaim,
How I love more than you; my pride would be
So great in having it divulg'd that I
Should fcarce (I am afraid) accept of life,
Tho' to enjoy you ftill.

   Phil. Come then, my dear,
Let's talk no more, but love, love till we die.

   Ara. Let's kill ourfelves with loving furioufly,
And fo prevent my father's future crimes. [*Exeunt.*

     Enter Cleon, Agremont, Adelard.

   Cleon. But are you fure the King has fent for
     him?

   Adel. Yes; to the fcaffold; but the King muft
     know,
It is in vain for Kings to war with heav'n.

                        Cleon.

Cleon. You told us tho' the King would hear
    this fact
Examin'd in the chamber of the Princefs.

Adel. He meant fo once, now he has chang'd
    his mind.

Cleon. Come then, we'll fcuffle hard before he
    perifh.

Enter King *and a Guard.*

King. Gentlemen, who faw Prince Thrafomond ?

Agr. He's gone, and pleafe your Majefty, to
view the city, and the new platform, with fome
gentlemen attending on him.

King. Is the Princefs ready to bring her pri-
    foners out ?

Adel. I'll go fee.

King. Tell her, we ftay.

Cleon. King, you may be deceived yet ;
The head you aim at coft more fetting on
Than to be loft fo flightly.

Enter Meffenger.

Meff. Where's the King ?

King. Here.

Meff. Hafte, Sir, to your ftrength, and fave
    yourfelf,

                                        The

The city's in a mutiny, fearing for lord Philander.

King. Bid 'em go hang themfelves.

Cleon. O, brave countrymen!

Mutiny, my fine dear countrymen, mutiny!

Now my brave valiant foremen, fhew your
    weapons,

In honour of your miftreffes.

Enter Philander, Araminta, *and* Endymion.

King. How come Philander thus to be unbound?

End. He is as faft as wedlock, Sir, can bind
    him,

King. What means this riddle?

Ara. He's my hufband, Sir.

King Your hufband, fay you? Call the captain in,

That guard's the citadel; there you fhall have

Your nuptial joys together: hear, you gods,

From this time do I fhake all title off

Of father to this woman, this bafe woman;

And what there is of vengeance in a lion

Caft among dogs, or robb'd of his dear young;

The fame inforc'd more terrible, and with

A greater rage, expect from me.

Ara. Sir, by

That little life I've left to fwear by, there

Is

Is nothing that can ſtir me from myſelf:
What I have done, I never ſhall repent of,
For death can be no bug-bear now to me,
Since Thraſomond is not to be my headſman.

 Cleon. Sweet peace upon thy ſoul, thou worthy
  woman,
Whene'er thou dy'ſt; for this time I'll excuſe thee,.
Or be thy prologue.

 Phil. Sir, let me ſpeak next;
And let my dying words perſuade you more
Than my dull life has done: if you deſign,
Or wiſh a wrong to her ſweet innocence,
You are a tyrant, and a ſavage one;
The memory of all your better deeds
Shall be in water writ, but this in marble:
No chronicle ſhall ſpeak you, tho' your own,
But for the ſhame of men; no monument
(Tho' high and big as Pelion) ſhall be able
To cover this baſe murder: make it rich
With braſs, with pureſt gold, and ſhining jaſper,
Like pyramids, and lay on epitaphs,
Such as make great men gods; my little marble
(That only cloaths my aſhes, not my faults)
Shall far out-ſhine it: and for after iſſues,
Think not ſo madly of the heav'nly wiſdoms,

         That

That they will give you more for your mad rage
To cut off thus, unlefs it be fome fnake,
Or fomething like yourfelf, that in his birth
Shall ftrangle you : think of my father, King,
There was a fault; but I forgive it; let
That fin perfuade you to be careful of
Your matchlefs daughter : fpare but her dear life,
And I'll furrender you my own with joy ;
Tho' I confefs I now could wifh to live,
For I in her have all this world can give
To make me happy.

   Enter another Meffenger.

 Meff. Arm, Sir, quickly, or
'Twill be too late ; the city's up in arms,
Led by an old gray ruffin that has feiz'd
Upon Prince Thrafomond, and fwears he'll kill
Him, if Philander be not ftreight releas'd.

 King. A thoufand devils take 'em.

 Cleon. A thoufand bleffings on 'em, and on all
Will take their parts; I'm fure that I'll make one.

 King. Come, to the citadel ; I'll fee thefe fafe.

    [*Ex. with* Philander *and* Araminta.
And then cope with thefe burghers. Let the guard,
And all the gentlemen, give ftrong attendance.

       [*Exit.*
       Manent

Manent Cleon, Agremont, Adelard.

Agr. The city up! This was above our wifhes.

Cleon. I, and the marriage too; now by my life
This noble lady has deceiv'd us all:
A plague upon myfelf, a thoufand plagues,
For having fuch unworthy thoughts of her
Dear honour. Oh, how I could beat myfelf?
Pri'thee beat me, and I'll beat thee again,
For we had both one thought.

Agr. No, 'twill lofe time.

Cleon. Are your fwords fharp? Well my dear
countrymen, what d'ye lack? If you continue and
fall not back upon the firft broken fhin, I'll have
you chronicled and chronicled, and cut and chronicled, and all to be prais'd, and fung in fonnets
and new ballads, that all tongues fhall troul you
in *fæcula fæculorum*, my kind can-carriers.

Adel. What if a toy take 'em in th' heels now,
and they run all away, and cry the devil take the
hindmoft?

Cleon. Then the fame devil take the foremoft
too, and fouce him for his breakfaft; if they all
prove cowards, my curfes fly amongft them, and
be fpeeding. May they have Murrains reign, to
keep the gentlemen at home unbound in eafe
                                        freeze:

freeze : may the moths branch their velvets, and their filks only be worn before fore eyes. May their falfe lights undo 'em, and difcover preffes, holes, ftrains and oldnefs in their ftuffs, and make 'em fhop-rid. May they keep whores and horfes, and break ; and live mew'd up with necks of beef and turneps. May they have many children, and all ugly like the fathers. May they know no language, but that gibberifh they prattle to their parcels, unlefs it be the *Gothick Latin* they write in their bonds, and may they write that falfe, and lofe their debts.

Enter King.

King. A vengeance take 'em, what a hum they make !

They fwarm like bees, and (like them) buz together :

They have no fenfe of any thing but noife.

And therefore will not hear, but bawl ftill all At once.

Cleon. Oh my brave countrymen ! as I live I will not buy a pin from out your walls for this ; nay, you fhall cozen me too, and I'll thank you for't.

King.

King. There is no ftopping them, thy're grown
    fo ftrong,
Except they fee Philander ; one kind look
Of his would fend them home as tame as fheep :
To m thy're fierce as lions, and they've reafons
Why fhould I hope for help in my diftrefs,
That ne'er could pity any one alive ?
We think ourfelves fo far above mankind,
That 'tis beneath us to be juft or grateful:
Alas, my faults are numberlefs.

Cleon. Yes, and
Your virtues are fo too ; for you have none.

King. I fee I muft releafe him now : it goes
Againft my heart to do a virtuous act;
But there's no remedy. Whofe there ? Go bring
Philander hither.

Cleon. What can all this mean ?

                     [*Exit* Adelard.

King. Ah, if we Princes did confider well,
We are but men as frail as others are,
As fubject to misfortunes, and as mortal ;
That if the powers above had made us great,
'Tis that we fhould with juftice rule their people,
That nations were not born to make us fport,
But we to make them glorious, fafe, and happy ;

                          All

All our concerns the gods would favour more,
And men would all fuch Kings like gods adore.

Enter Agremont *and* Philander.

O worthy Sir, forgive me ; do not make
Both my offences, and your wrongs combine
To bring on greater dangers ; be yourfelf,
Still found among difeafes ; if I've done
You injury, I'll make you now amends ;
Calm but the people, and my daughter's your's ;
Take her, and with her my repentance, Sir,
My wifhes, and my prayers : you fhall be
What you was born to be, King of this land.
Do not miftruft me ; if the leaft untruth
Fall from me now, may I be ftruck with thunder.
    Phil. I will not do your Majefty the wrong
To doubt your word ; let but the Princefs, and
The boy be free, and I will ftand alone
The fhock of all this rabble ; which I'll quell
Or perifh in the attempt.
    King. Your word already
Has done that : go fetch 'em hither ftraight.
    Phil. Then thus I take my leave, kiffing your
        hand,
And trufting to your royal promife, Sir,
    Vol. II.   H   Be

Be not difturb'd : I'll bring you back the peace
You wifh for.

King. All the gods attend upon you.   [*Exeunt.*

Enter an Old Captain *and* Citizens *with* Thrafomond.

Cap. Come, my brave Myrmidons, let's fall on,
    let our caps
Swarm, my boys, and your nimble tongues forget
    your mother's
Gibberifh of, ' What do you lack,' and fet your
    mouths
Up, children, till your palates fall frighted half a
Fathom paft the cure of bay falt and grofs pepper,
And then cry, Philander, brave Philander,
Let Philander be deeper in requeft, my ding-dongs,
My pair of dear indentures, king of clubs,
Than your cold water chamblets, or your paintings
Spitted with copper; let not your hafty filks,
Or your branch'd cloth of bodkin, or your tiffues,
Dearly beloved of fpice cake and cuftard,
Your Robin Hoods and Johns, tie your affections
In darknefs to your fhops; no, dainty duckers;
Up with your three-pil'd fpirits, your wrought
    valours,

                                    And

And let your uncouth choler make the King feel
The meafure of your mightinefs.   Philander,
Cry, my rofe-nobles, cry.

   All. Philander, Philander.

   Cap. How do you like this, my lord Prince ?
      thefe are mad boys,

I tell you thefe are things that will not ftrike their
      top-fails

To a foift, and let a man of war, an Argofie, hull
      and cry cockles.

   Thraf. Why, you rude flaves, do you know what
you do ?

   Cap. My pretty Prince of puppets, we do know,
And give your greatnefs warning that you talk
No more fuch bug's words, or that folder'd crown
Shall be fcratch'd with a mufquet : dear Prince
      Pepin,

Down with your noble blood, or as I live
I'll have you coddled.   Let him loofe, my fpirits ;
Make a round ring with your bills, my Hectors,
And let us fee what this trim man dares do.
Now, Sir, have at you ; here I hit you,
And with this fwafhing blow, (do you fweat Prince ?)
I could hulk your grace, and hang you up crofs-
      legg'd,

H 2

Like

Like a hare at the poulterer's, and do this with
    this viper.

Thraf. You will not fee me murder'd, wicked
    villains ?

1 *Cit.* Yes indeed will we, Sir, we have not feen
    one fo this great while.

Cap. He would have weapons, would he? Give
him a broadfide, my brave boys, with your pikes;
branch me his fkin in flowers like a fatin, and between every flower a mortal cut; your royalty
fhall ravel; jagg him gentlemen. I'll have him
cut to the keel, and down the feams: oh for a
whip to make him galoon laces: I'll have a coach
whip.

Thraf. O, fpare me, gentlemen.

Cap. Hold, hold, the man begins to fear, and
    know himfelf,

He fhall, for this time, only be feal'd up
With a feather thro' his nofe, that he may only fee
Heav'n, and think whither he's a-going;
Nay (beyond fea, Sir,) we will proclaim you, you
    would be King?
Thou tender heir apparent to church ale,
Thou flight Prince of fingle farcenet;
Thou royal ring-tail, fit to fly at nothing

2

But

But poor men's poultry, and have every boy
Beat thee from that too with his bread and butter.

 Thraf. Gods! keep me from thefe hell-hounds·

 2 *Cit.* Shall's geld him, captain?

 Cap. No, you fhall fpare his dowcets, my dear
  donfels,
As you refpect the ladies, let them flourifh:
The curfes of a longing woman kills as fpeedily as a
Plague, boys.

 1 *Cit.* I'll have a leg, that's certain.

 2 *Cit.* I'll have an arm.

 3 *Cit.* I'll have his nofe, and at my own charge
build a college, and clap't upon the gate.

 4 *Cit.* I'll have his little gut to ftring a kite with;
For certainly a royal gut will found like filver.

 5 *Cit.* Good captain, let me have his liver to
feed ferrets.

 Cap. Who will have parcels elfe? Speak.

 Thraf. Good gods, confider me; I fhall be tor-
  tur'd.

 1 *Cit.* Captain, I'll give you the trimming of
your hand-fword, and let me have his fkin to make
falfe fcabbards.

 2 *Cit.* He had no horns, Sir, had he?

H 3

Cap.

Cap. No, Sir, he's a pollard. What would'ft thou do with horns?

2 *Cit.* Oh! if he had, I would have made rare hafts and whiftles of them, but his ſhin bones, if they be found, will ſerve me well enough.

Enter Philander.

All. Long live Philander! the brave Prince Philander.

Phil. I thank you, gentlemen, but why are theſe Rude weapons brought abroad to teach your hands Uncivil trades?

Cap. My royal roficcleer,
We are thy myrmidons, thy guards, thy roarers;
And when this noble body is in durance,
Thus do we clap our mufty murry on,
And trace the ſtreets in terror. Is it peace,
Thou mars of men? Is the King ſociable,
And bids thee live? Art thou above thy foe, man?
And free as Phœbus? Speak; if not, this ſtand
Of royal blood ſhall be a-broach, a tilt, and run
Ev'n to the lees of honour.

Phil. Hold, and be ſatisfy'd, I am myſelf
Free as my thoughts are, by the gods I am.

Cap.

Cap. Art thou the dainty darling of the King?
Art thou the Hylas to our Hercules?
Do the Lords bow, and the regarded scarlets,
Kiss their gam'd goles, and cry we are your ser-
  vants?
Is the court navigable, and the presence stuck
With flags of friendship? If not, we are thy castle,
And this man sleeps.

 Phil. I am what I desire to be, your friend,
I am what I was born to be, your Prince.
And what, Sir, say you now!

 Thras. For God's sake set me first free, and I'll
say any thing; I am so afraid I know not what to
say,

 Phil. I do pity thee. Friends discharge your
  fears,
Deliver me the Prince. I'll warrant you
I shall be old enough to find my safety.

 Cap. Prince, by your leave, I'll have a surfiagle,
And make you like a hawk.

 Phil. Away, away, there is no danger in him:
Look you, friends, how gently he leads; upon
  my word
He's tame enough, he needs no farther watching:
Good friends, go to your houses, and by me have

      Your

Your pardons and my love.
And know there shall be nothing in my pow'r
You may deserve, but you shall have your wishes.
To give you more thanks were to flatter you :
Continue still your love, and, for an earnest,
Die with this.

    All. Long may'st thou live, brave Prince, brave
      Prince, brave Prince.

          [*Exit* Philander *and* Thrasomond.
Cap. Thou art the King of courtesy.
Fall off again, my sweet youths, and every man
trace to his house again, and hang his pewter up,
thence to the tavern, and bring your wives in
muffs ; we will have music, and red grape shall
make us dance and reel, boys.   [*Ex. omnes.*

Enter King, Araminta, Melesinda, Alga, Cleon,
  Agremont, Adelard, Endymion, *and attendants.*

   King. Is it appeas'd ?
   Cleon. Sir, all is quiet as this dead of night,
As peaceable as sleep. The lord Philander
Does bring Prince Thrasomond away himself.

    King. I will not break a word that I have giv'n
In promise to him : I have heap'd a world

                       Of

Of grief upon his head, which yet I hope
To wafh away.

Enter Philander *and* Thrafomond.

Cleon. My lord is come.

King. My fon,
Bleft be the time that I of right do call
Such virtue mine. Now thou art in my arms,
Methinks I find a falve to my fick bofom
For all the wounds I find there : ftreams of grief
I have thrown on thee, but I find much joy,
That I repent it, iffue from my eyes.
Let them appeafe thee, take thy right, take her,
She is thy right too, and forget to urge
My vexed foul for what I once have done.

Phil. Sir, all is blotted from my memory :
For you, young Prince of Spain,
Whom I have thus redeem'd, you have full leave
To make your honourable voyage home.
And if you would go furnifh'd to your realm
With fair diverfion, I do fee a lady
Methinks would bear you company.
How like you, Sir, this piece ?

Alga. Sir, he likes it well,
For he has try'd it, and found it worth

His

His Princely liking.   We were ta'en a-bed,
I know your meaning.   I am not the first
That nature taught to seek a handsome fellow.
Can shame remain perpetually in me,
And not in others ? Or have Princes salves
To cure ill names, that meaner people want ?

   Phil. What mean you ?

   Alga. You must get another ship
To bear the Princess and the boy together.

   Cleon. How now ?

   Alga. Others took me, but I took her and him,
As that all women may be ta'en sometimes,
Ship us all four ; we can endure
Weather and wind alike.

   King. Clear then thyself, or call me not thy
      father.

   Ara. 'Tis false as heaven is true; but what means
Is left to clear myself? It lies in your belief.
My lords, believe me, and let all things else
Struggle together to dishonour me.

   End. O ! stop your ears, great King, that I may
      speak
As freedom would, then I will call this lady
As base as are her actions: hear me, Sir,

                         Believe

Believe your heated blood when it rebels
Againſt your reaſon, ſooner than this lady.

Alga. I vow the boy acts his part full well.

Phil. This lady; I will ſooner truſt the winds
or ſeas

Than her. I ſay believe her not.
Why think you if I did believe her words,
I would outlive them?

King. Forget her; ſince all is firm between us;
But I muſt requeſt of you one favour,
And will not be deny'd.

Phil. By all the powers let it not be the death
Of her or him, and it is ſurely granted.

King. Bear away that boy
To torture, I will have her clear'd or bury'd.

Phil. O give my promiſe back, O royal Sir,
Aſk ſomething elſe, bury my life and right
In one poor grave; but take not from me
My life and fame at once.

King. Away with him; his doom's irrevocable.

Phil. Turn all your eyes on me, here ſtands a
man, .

The falſeſt and the baſeſt of the world.
Set ſwords againſt this breaſt, ſome honeſt man.
For I have liv'd to be the moſt accurs'd.

I   *End.*

End. Be patient, Sir, I foon will make you eafy.
I cannot tamely fee your pain for me ;
My haplefs fortune much rather I'll reveal.

 King. Will he then confefs ?

 Cleon. He feems to fay fo.

 King. Speak then.

 End. Great King, if you command
This lord to talk with me alone, my tongue
Urg'd by my heart, fhall utter all the thoughts
My youth has known, and ftranger things than
  thefe
You hear not often.

 King. Walk afide with him.

 Cleon. Why fpeak'ft thou not ?

 End. Know you this face, my lord ?

 Cleon. No.

 End. I have been often told
In court of one Euphrofyne, a lady,
And daughter to you, between whom and me
There was fuch ftrange refemblance, that we two
Could not be known afunder, dreft alike.

 Cleon. By heav'n, and fo there is.

 End. For her fake,
Who now does fpend the fpring-time of her life
In holy pilgrimage, move the King,

         That

That I may 'fcape this torture.

Cleon. But thou fpeak'ft as like Euphrofyne as
thou doft look.
How came it to thy knowledge that fhe lives
In pilgrimage?

End. I know it not, my lord, but have heard it,
And do fcarce believe it.

Cleon. Oh my fhame! Is't poffible? Draw near,
That I may gaze upon thee? Art thou fhe,
Or elfe her murderer? Where waft thou born?

End. In Syracufe.

Cleon. What's thy name?

End. Euphrofyne.

Cleon. 'Tis fhe!
Now do I know thee? Oh, that thou had'ft dy'd,
And I had never feen thee, nor my fhame!
How fhall I own thee? fhall this tongue of mine
E'er call thee daughter more?

End. Would I had dy'd indeed; I wifh it too,
E'er publifh'd what I have told;
But that there was no means
To hide it longer; yet I joy in this,
The Princefs is all clear.

King. What have you done?

Cleon. All is difcover'd.

Ara. What is difcover'd?

Cleon.

Cleon. Why my fhame.
It is a woman, let her fpeak the reft.

    Phil. How! that again.

    Cleon. It is a woman.   [*Exit.*

    Phil. Bleft be the pow'rs that favour innocence.

    King. Lay hold upon that lady.

    Phil. It is a woman; hark ye, gentlemen,
It is a woman! Araminta, take
My foul into thy breaft, that could be gone
With joy! It is a woman; thou art fair
And virtuous ftill to ages, in defpight of malice.

    King. Speak you, where lies his fhame?

    End. I am his daughter.

    Phil. The gods are juft.

    Cleon. I dare accufe none; but before you two
The virtue of the age, I bend my knee
For mercy.

    Phil. Take it freely; for I know
It was well meant.

    Ara. And for me,
I have the will to pardon fins as oft
As any man has power to wrong me.

    Cleon. Noble and worthy!

    Phil. But, Endymion,
(For I muft call thee ftill fo) tell me why

                         Thou

Thou didſt conceal thy ſex ? It was a fault,
A fault, Endymion, though thy other deeds
Of truth outweigh'd it.   All theſe jealouſies
Had flown to nothing, if thou hadſt diſcover'd
What now we know.

   End. My father oft would ſpeak
Your worth and virtue with a zealous praiſe,
Which, as I grew in age, increas'd a thirſt
Of ſeeing of a man ſo rais'd above the reſt.
But this was but the child of curioſity,
Till fate one day brought you to my father's,
And I was order'd there to entertain you.
Oh ſpare my bluſhes; and yet a flame ſo pure
Methinks ſhould cauſe no ſhame.
The only bliſs that ever I propos'd,
Was ſtill to live and be within your ſight.
For this I did delude my noble father
With a feign'd pilgrimage, and dreſt myſelf
In a boy's habit, and underſtanding well,
That when I made diſcovery of my ſex
I could not ſtay with you, I made a vow,
By all the moſt religious things a maid
Could call together, never to be known,
Whilſt there was hopes to hide me from men's eyes,
For other than I ſeem'd, that I might ever

                                        Abide

Abide with you.   Then fat I by the fountain,
Where firft you took me up.

   King. Search out a match,
Greateft in our kingdoms, and I will
Pay thy dower myfelf.

   End. Ne'er, Sir, will I
Marry, it is a thing within my vow:
But if I may have leave to ferve the Princefs,
To fee the virtues of her lord and her,
I fhall have hopes to live.

   Ara. Yes, Philander,
I can't be jealous, tho' you had a lady
Dreft like a page to ferve you; nor will I
Sufpect her living here.   Come, live with me,
Live free as I do; fhe that loves my lord,
Curft be the wife that hates her.

   Phil. I grieve fuch virtue fhould be laid in earth
Without an heir.   Hear me, my royal father,
Wrong not the freedom of our foul fo much,
To think to take revenge on this bafe woman:
Her malice cannot hurt us; fet her free
As fhe was born, faving from fhame and fin.

   King. Set her at liberty: but leave the court;
This is no place for fuch.   You, Thrafomond,
Shall have free paffage, and fafe conduct home,
Worthy

Worthy fo great a Prince. When you come there,
Remember 'twas your fault that coft you here
And not my purpos'd will.

    Thraf. I do confefs it, moft renowned Sir.

    King. Laft join your hands in one ; enjoy Phi-
       lander,

This kingdom that is yours, and after me
Whatever I call mine ; my blefling on you :
All happy hours be at your marriage joys,
That you may govern all thefe happy lands,
And live to fee your plenteous branches fpring.
By what has paft this day let Princes learn
To rule the wilder paffions of their blood,
For what heav'n wills can never be withftood.

THE

E P · I L O G U E.

TO BE SPOKEN BY THE GOVERNOR.

IF by my deep contrivance, wit and fkill,
'Things fall out crofs to what I mean them ftill,
You muft not wonder ; 'tis the commmon fate
Of almoft all grave governors of late :
And one would fwear, as every plot has fped,
They thought more with their elbows than their
      head ;
Yet they go on as brifk, and look as well,
As if they had out-wifdom'd Machiavel :
So curs will wag their tails, and think they've
      won us,
At the fame inftant they make water on us.
Is't not to let us fee men fhould have none,
That have fuch tedious, fulfome bungling fhown ;
For to go five years wrong, with art and pains,
Does fhew a moft prodigious want of brains ;
Nay tho' he ne'er judg'd right, yet there was one ⎫
Who bragadocied ftill himfelf upon   ⎬
Being infallible, but he is gone.   ⎭

                        O ! 'twas

O ! 'twas a thought of vaſt deſign and ſcope,
To rail ſtill againſt popery and hope,
He might preſume to be himſelf a Pope:

Tho' he might any thing preſume to be,
That could deceive fops ſo infallibly ;
The moſt egregious of all ſcribes could tell,
There never was ſuch an Ahitophel :
And true admirers of his parts and glory
Will doubtleſs have a juſt renown in ſtory,
Ten guineas that lord paid for't, as fame goes,
Above ten times its worth the world knows ;
But he'll be better paid yet, I ſuppoſe.

They were a matchleſs pair, the one to plot,
The other to extol ſtill what was not.
Yet, faith, the little lord, when hence he ran,
Did compaſs one thing like an able man :
For, ſince he could not living act with reaſon,
'Twas ſhrewdly done of him to die in ſeaſon.

THE

THE

BATTLE OF SEDGMOOR:

BETWIXT

KING JAMES'S FORCES

AND THE

DUKE OF MONMOUTH,

REHEARSED AT WHITEHALL.

A FARCE.

DRAMATIS PERSONÆ.

The General, a Frenchman *, that commanded
King James's forces at the battle againſt the
Duke of Monmouth, in the Weſt.
A Nobleman of England.
An Engliſh Lady.

Scene, a Drawing Room in Whitehall.

* Lewis de Duras, Marquis of Blanquefort, brother to
the Duke de Duras, in France, and nephew of Marſhal
Turenne, was naturalized by Act of Parliament, 17
Charles II. and behaving with great gallantry in the war
with the Dutch, was created Baron Duras of Holdenby, in
Com. Northampton. He married Mary the eldeſt of the
two daughters and coheirs to George Sondes, Earl of Fe-
verſham, in whoſe right, according to the entail, he came
to enjoy that Earldom. He dying in 1709 without iſſue,
the title became extinct.

THE

BATTLE OF SEDGMOOR*;

SCENE, *A Drawing Room in Whitehall.*

Enter a Lord *and a* Lady.

Lady. DID you ever hear of fuch a thing as this battle, as they call it ?

Lord. Not I, I'll be fworn, nor no man elfe I think.

Lady. Every body fays, that as the bufinefs was order'd, it was a thoufand to one but all the King's forces had been cut off,

Lord. Yes, that is moft certain ; but that I am moft delighted with is, to fee the infinite fatisfaction the General takes in explaining to every one he meets with, all the particulars of his foolery.

Lady. O! here he is a coming; for God fake let us make him tell it us again.

Lord. Pray do, Madam,

---

* The King ordered the regulars and guards to march againft Monmouth, under the command of the Earl of Feverfham, an honeft, brave, and good-natured Nobleman; but he conducted matters fo ill, that every ftep he made was like to prove fatal to the King's fervice. He had no parties abroad, he got no intelligence, and was almoft furprized, and like to be defeated, when he feemed to be under no apprehenfions, but was a-bed, without any care or order. The Earl was weak in his underftanding, and his vanity has fubjected him to the ridicule of the Duke of Buckingham.

Enter

Enter General.

Gener. Madama, your moſt humble ſervanta.

Lady. Whither are you going ſo faſt, my Lord?

Gener. Madama, me be going about ſome buſi-neſs of very grand importaunce.

Lady. But my Lord, will not you tell us a little firſt, ſome of the particulars of this battle?

Gener. Madama, vid all min harta, me tell a you begarra de hola hiſtoria o'de occaſion: your Ladiſhip have hear, I ſuppoſa, dat de rebella get into the great towna-----Vat you call de towna?

Lady. What, Briſtol?

Gener. No, de oder towna.

Lord. Exeter?

Gener. No, no, a pox take de towna vid de hard name: How you call de towna, de Breech?

Lady. Lord have mercy upon me, what does he mean?

Lord. Nay, I cannot imagine.

Lady. O! Bridgwater.

Gener. Ay begarra, Breechwater; ſo madama me have intelligenſa dat de rebel go to Breech-water; me ſay to my mena, marſh you rogua; ſo me marſha over de greata fielda, begar, de brava contra were dey killa de hare vid de dogua, and the patrich vid de hawka, begar, de brave ſport in de varld.

Lord. Well, my Lord, and what then?

Gener. Begar me marſh very well vid de drome and de trumpetra, de drombela and de great noiſa begar; au how you call de brave fellow au de fine cappa turn ope vid de great poucha o'de ſide?

Lord.

Lord. Who, the granadier?

Gener. Ay begar, de granadere vid de hoboya, begar, de fine mufick in de varld.

Lady. But, my Lord, what did you do there?

Gener. Why madama, me come vid in two mile o' Breechwater, and begarra, me poft my felf dere.

Lord. How many men, pray, my Lord, were there of the rebels?

Gener. Ma foy, between fixa and fevena toufand.

Lord. How many had you?

Gener. Abouta two toufand.

Lady. But, my Lord, if you were fo few; why would you come fo near the enemy?

Gener. Begarra, madama, becaufe me no care for de enemia.

Lord. I fuppofe, my Lord, that your Lordfhip was pofted in a very ftrong place.

Gener. O begarra very ftrong, vid de great river between me and de rebella, calla, de Brooka de Gutter.

Lady. But they fay, my Lord, there was no water in that Brook of the Gutter.

Gener. Begar, madama, but dat no be my faulta, begar me no hander de water from coma, if no will rain, begar me no can make de rain.

Lady. But why did you not go to fome other place?

Gener. O pardon me, madama, you no under-ftand de ting.

Lord. And fo your Lordfhip, it feems, encamp'd with your horfe and foot.

Gener.

Gener. Ay, vid de foota; no, vid de horfa, begar me go vid de horfa an de gentlemen officera to one very good villafh, where, begar, be very good quartera, very good meta, very good drinka, and very good bedda.

Lady. But pray, my Lord, why did you not ftay with the foot ?

Gener. Begarra, madama, becaufe dere be great differentia between de gentlemen officera and de rogua de fogiera; begarra, de rogua de fogiera lye upon de grounda; but begar, de gentleman officera go to bedda.

Lady. But, my Lord, tho' by your favour, you would have been more fecure, if you had been together.

Gener. Begarra, madama, you no underftan de art militair.

Lord. Well, my Lord, how it was done is no great matter ; but, God be prais'd, it feems they are beaten.

Gener. Beata ! Ay, begar, dey be very well beata : Begar, me beata dem, and me killa dem like de rogua.

Lady. You beat 'em ! How could you beat 'em, when you were not there ?

Gener. Begar, madama, but they were beata by my ordera.

Lady. How by your order ?

Gener. Why, begar, madama, before me go to bedda, me make to dem one very good fpeecha.

Lord. Ay; pray, my Lord, let us hear : What is it you faid to them ?

Gener. Begar, my Lore, me come to dem vid de great
golda

golda fcarfa, begar very fine, vid a new pirrewigga
begar very handfom, and, a brave beaver hatta;
begar me coka de hatta, an look to dem as big as
de divel: Vid all de gentleman officera behinda
me, and begar all very fina. So de fogiera giva
de great fhouta, and cry, God blefs our Generalla,
God blefs your Excelenfa; an alla dofe tinga dat
fho de refpect an de lova to de perfon o'de qualite.
So me fay to dem, harka, you rogua de fogiera,
me be your Generalla; me be a kin to my coufin,
the Marfhal Turena, de great General in de varld;
begar he fho me all de trick 'o de warra, an all de
poleteca; begar me tella you derefore one tinga:
Begarra, if you ftir from de camp, you rogua de
fogiera, begarra me hanga you by de law marti-
alla; an marka you me one ting more, when de
rebella coma, fhoota de mufqueta, fhoot de great
gonn, make de great noifa, an begar when de
rebella runna, kill de rogua vid the pike in de
back, and de bullet in de narfa.

Lady. O, was that then the orders you gave
them? Your fervant, my Lord,   [*Exit* Lady.

Lord. Nay, if your Lordfhip faid that, you did
all that a man could do.

Gener. Begar me know dat very wella: Begar
me no come here to learna de art militaira; begar
me de teacha dat very wella in my own contria.
But, my Lore, begar me tella you one hiftoria
will make you laffa: begar de nit o' de batalla me
be in bed vid one very pretty womans; begar, my
Lore, de taut o' de occafione o' de mufketa, o' de
cannona, o' de pika, de bullet an de fworda, be-
                                        gar

gar fo run in my heada, dat begar me could do tinga.

Lord. Ay, my Lord, I don't doubt of that. Your Lordſhips moſt humble ſervant. [*Exit.* Lord.

Gener. Begar now dis be one very pretty tinga : Me beata de enemy like de great Generalla, like de man o'de conducta, an begar becauſa me no born in Englanda, begar de Engliſhman laff at me. Odſooner, dey be de ſtrangia natioon in de varld.   [*Exit.*

MILITANT COUPLE:

OR, THE

HUSBAND MAY THANK HIMSELF.

A

DRAMATIC DIALOGUE.

Freeman. WELL! If thefe are the bleffed effects of marriage, the Lord keep me and all good Chriftians, I fay, out of the pale of matrimony :----But pr'ythee, Bellair, is this their conftant courfe of life?

Bellair. Why really, yes. Only with this difference, that what thou faw'ft yefterday, was nothing but meer fport and paftime to the terrible tragedies I have feen.

Freeman. For my part, I can't comprehend how the fcene cou'd poffibly be worfe. Methinks Sir John and my Lady threw whore and rogue at one another very plentifully.

Bellair. Pfhaw, pfhaw, cuftom and ufe have made thofe words fo familiar to them, that now they have loft all the poignancy of their fignification. Alas! 'twas a meer calm, if compared to what tempeftuous bluftering weather I have feen in the family. Thou may'ft as well think there runs as high a fea in Chelfea Reach, as in the Bay of Bifcay, as conclude from yefterday's bickering-

what

what noble exploits are done among 'em, when both fides are heroically inclin'd.

Freeman. I fubmit, fince there's no difputing againft matter of fact. However, pray inform me, what can be worfe than what I beheld yefterday? Can any thing be more provoking, than for a man to infult his wife after that mercilefs rate; or more odious, than for a woman to expofe her hufband's infirmities?

Bellair. Yes, I tell you, blows are more provoking and odious. What fignify a few foolifh angry words? they don't break bones, nor give black eyes. Befides, as I told you before, this fort of language is now become fo habitual to this worthy couple, that it makes no manner of impreffion upon them. Mithridates, you know, by accuftoming himfelf to poifon, brought his body to fuch a pitch at laft, that he could regale himfelf with opium, and feaft upon ratfbane.

Freeman So hiftorians fay indeed. 'Tis true, with the generality of conftitutions, blows go a great deal farther than words. But, does Sir John beftow fuch favours often upon my lady?

Bellair. I have feen him deliver her over to the fecular arm more than once. I remember, I dined there laft winter, by the fame token a quarrel happen'd about drefling of a difh of fifh. Sir John fwore the cook deferved to be crucified for fpoiling fo noble a brace of carp. My lady, juftified him, faid the fauce was of her own ordering, and rallied Sir John very pleafantly upon the vicioufnefs of his palate.

Freeman.

I

Freeman. Why, this is neither better nor worfe than what I have feen in moft families.

Bellair. This nettled Sir John wonderfully, who you muft know values himfelf upon the ortho-doxy of his tafte. After abundance of good-na-tured compliments had paft between 'em upon this head, Yes, madam, fays he, I muft own you are in the right: my palate is very vicious, and I fhow'd it with a witnefs, when I married fuch a compofition of pride, malice, and luft, as your ladyfhip.

Freeman. Ah, worthy knight, that was fpoke like a hero! but what reply did my lady make to it?

Bellair. At leaft, fays fhe, I have fomething more to plead for myfelf than thou haft. I knew thee to be a worthlefs fot, an empty, guzzling, fmoaking wretch. But a villain of an uncle, whom I hope the devil has rewarded for his pains, forced me to take thee for my hufband; otherwife I had fooner courted an infection, and bedded a leprofy, than fuffered myfelf to be polluted with thy naufeous embraces.

Freeman. The true fpirit of an Amazon, upon my word.

Bellair. I thought, 'twas now high time to in-terpofe between the knight and his lady; fo addrefling myfelf to Sir John, I told him, that women had their odd fancies fometimes, which a wife man ought to connive at: then turning to my lady, I reprefented to her the duty of her fex; but finding that my preaching up of peace and moderation rather aggravated matters, than fof-
ten'd

ten'd them, I refolved to fit ftill, and leave all to the over-ruling wifdom of Providence.

Freeman. A very chriftian difpofition. But proceed,

Bellair. The cloth was no fooner removed, but the war broke out with greater fury than ever. Sir John extreamly provoked at fomething my lady had faid to him, fwore and blufter'd like a hero in one of our modern tragedies. My lady, on her fide, exercifed her lungs with equal vigour, and was no lefs obftreperous. At laft the knight, unable to contain himfelf any longer, ftruck off her commode, which courtefy her ladyfhip immediately requited, by throwing Sir John's perriwig upon the fire.

Freeman. This was doing bufinefs to fome purpofe.

Bellair. With that Sir John pufhes my lady againft a fine new pendulum-clock, that ftood in the room, and broke the olive cafe all to pieces. My lady foon rallied and beat back Sir John upon a huge Japan looking-glafs, which was demolifh'd in an inftant; to retaliate which favour, the knight finifhed all her china at three or four ftrokes of his cane. But now they came to a clofer engagement, diftributing their blows to one another with incredible gallantry, while I-----

Freeman. That is, what I long to hear; for methinks I wou'd have found myfelf *un peu embaraffé* how to behave myfelf in fo nice a conjuncture.

Bellair.

Bellair. Liften then.   All this while I fate un-concern'd upon my chair, keeping up to my old maxim of being neuter, between the two con-tending crowns.   At laft, after an hours difpute, tho' with fome fhort intermiffions, heaven was pleafed to declare itfelf in favour of my lady, who retired triumphantly out of the parlour, and left her lord and mafter groveling upon the floor with a brace of black eyes; and all this to fhew the vehemence of her affection.

Freeman. Well! 'tis a myftery to me, that married people, however they behave themfelves to one another in private, fhou'd not take care to preferve a fair outfide at leaft before ftrangers. I knew a gentleman and his wife, who treated one another in public with all the refpect and civility that can be imagined, fo that you'd fwear they were the moft affectionate couple that ever graced the ftate of matrimony, fince the concate-nation of Adam and Eve in Paradife.   But when they were by themfelves the cafe was alter'd, and they fhow'd themfelves in their proper fhapes.----- But prithee Bellair how long have Sir John and my Lady been married?

Bellair. Somewhat better than five years.   Sir John was the fame numerical beaft then you be-hold him now: but my Lady one of the moft agreeable, fweet temper'd creatures the fun ever faw, and if fhe's alter'd for the worfe, Sir John may e'en thank his own ill management.   Alas! I know the whole hiftory of their inteftine broils, and what occafion'd them.   I was invited to the wedding.

VOL. II.   K   *Freeman.*

Freeman. And what did you obferve remarkable at this ceremony?

Bellair. Nothing as I know of, but what happens at all weddings. There was a world of noife and impertinence, of fcandal and bawdy, attended with dancing, fiddling, fwearing, drinking, fmoaking, and the like. One thing indeed was fomewhat particular: the bride's brother, who is a true country rake, without the leaft fhare of good fenfe, or manners to atone for his vices, was pleas'd to tell all the company, how he had confummated (but he ufed a more familiar ex-preffion for't) the night before with a farmer's daughter upon a hay-cock; and this he delivered in fuch beaftly language, that I wonder none of the grave ancient matrons at the table did not rebuke him for't.

Freeman. Why marriages, you know, are like the feafts of Saturn, devoted to merriment and liberty, and as in the latter, flaves were permitted to fit down with their mafters; fo in the former, the language of flaves (for what better name does obfcenity deferve) is allow'd, I can't tell why, to come for a fhare.

Bellair. The parfon of the parifh led up the dances all the afternoon in his caffock, for both the weather and fport were too hot for him to whifk it about in all his ecclefiaftical harnefs. But what makes me dwell upon fuch infignificant trifles as thefe? In four days all the company parted, and had Sir John been a man of tolerable difcretion, he would certainly have been the happieft man in the univerfe. But I confefs, his behaviour

haviour upon the nuptial day, gave me a vile omen of his future conduct.

Freeman. Why, what was that?

Bellair. Inftead of faving himfelf from the bottle (which any man of common fenfe in his circumftances would have done) he muft needs vifit every company in the houfe, and like a northern inn-keeper, drank with all his guefts; fo that when he came to bed to his bride, he was as drunk as a chaplain of the army upon wetting his commiffion; and ftunk of tobacco worfe than a foot-foldier, that breakfafts, dines, and fups upon the weed.

Freeman. This was foolifh enough. However, this may be faid in Sir John's excufe, that the day of marriage being a day of hurry and tumult, 'tis no wonder if the perfon chiefly concerned in all this came to fuffer by it firft. Befides, I need not tell you that 'tis the wicked way of this world for the men to combine againft the bridegroom on thefe occafions, in order to difable him from paying the tribute of the marriage-bed.

Bellair. For this very reafon, Freeman, a man ought to fet a double guard upon himfelf, and avoid the train that is laid to blow him up.

Freeman. That's right, but a fpirit of good-nature and hofpitality may fometimes carry a man beyond the rules of decorum. Well, but if Sir John made this falfe ftep upon the day of marriage, I hope he has made amends for it fince.

Bellair. Why truly, if continuing one fault with another, is making amends for't, I know no man in the three kingdoms that has made more

fubftantial

substantial amends than Sir John. In short, he minded his dogs, his cocks, his horses, &c. more than his lady; was seldom or ever at home; and when he was, such a litter of scoundrels still accompanied him, there was such a squabbling about the merits of Thunder and Ringwood, such a profusion of groundless calumny and scandal, that a woman of any breeding would much rather submit to sit out three naked prizes at the Beargarden, than be forced to do penance in this nauseous ribbaldry.

Freeman. And yet a woman must endure these hardships as well as she can, since the generality of our country-gentlemen inure them to't.

Bellair. Never tell me what the generality of brutes do. Don't you think a fine woman, in the bloom of her age, that has brought a noble fortune into a family, if she has any spirit or resentment of injuries, must not abominate the stupid, ungrateful sot that neglects and slights her, that prefers the company of the vilest scoundrels to hers; that can hardly afford her a civil word when he's sober, and always insults her when he's drunk? Don't you think, I say, that a woman must have something very angelical in her constitution, not to retaliate upon her husband that uses her thus, when an opportunity is offered her?

Freeman. I' faith I must own 'tis insupportable usage; and if I were a woman, and treated so barbarously, for all the christianity I pretend to, I am afraid, I should rebel.

Bellair.

Bellair. To return now to my difcourfe from which thefe reflections have infenfibly led me. Sir John was generally abroad at his cock-matches and horfe-races, projecting Newmarket affignations, tippling with his brother juftices of the peace, managing elections, punifhing the interlopers upon game, while his lady lived as melancholy a life at home, as if fhe had been confined to a nunnery; with this improvement too of her perfecution, that fhe had nothing to converfe with, but an old, affected, malicious aunt of Sir John, who continually entertain'd her with dull infipid hiftories of the heroes and heroines of her family.

Freeman. And how did fhe bear it?

Bellair. With a patience hardly to be parallel'd. I know fome malicious people in the neighbourhood talk ftrange things of a private intrigue between her and a certain gentleman, with which they have fo effectually poffeffed the knight, that this has occafion'd all the ill blood between them; tho' I can't imagine what pretence Sir John has to be jealous; for why fhould a man be jealous, that never was capable of love; or be concern'd to have that property invaded, which he always flighted?

Freeman. As ill an opinion as I have of the fair fex, yet I believe their mifcarriages, generally fpeaking, are purely owing to the men. A ftate muft be troubled with civil diffentions at home, before any foreigner will pretend to invade it; and there muft be an ill underftanding between

K 3 the

the wife and the hufband, before a gallant can hope to fucceed in the family.

Bellair. After all, if the lady has actually tref-paſs'd againſt Sir John's honour, the Knight has none to thank but himſelf; for let a huſband be never fo much the ſuperior, and flatter himſelf never fo much with an imaginary pre-eminence, yet if he affects a defpotic ſway, takes more upon him than the law allows him, and violates the original contract, 'tis as natural for wives as for ſubjects to rebel.

POEMS,

P O E M S.

DEATH OF THE LORD FAIRFAX,

DUTCHESS DOWAGER OF BUCKINGHAM.

UNDER this ftone does lie
One born for victory;
FAIRFAX the viliant, and the only he,
Whoe'er for that alone a conqueror wou'd be :
Both fexes virtues were in him combin'd ;
He had the fiercenefs of the manlieft mind,
And yet the meeknefs too of woman-kind :
He never knew what envy was, nor hate ;
   His foul was fill'd with truth and honefty,
And with another thing, quite out of date, call'd
     modefty.

II.

He ne'er feem'd impudent, but in the place
   Where impudence itfelf dares feldom fhew its
     face ;
Had any ftrangers fpy'd him in the room
   With fome of thofe he had overcome,
And had not heard their talk, but only feen
Their gefture and their mein,
They wou'd have fworn he had the vanquifh'd
     been :
For as they bragg'd, and dreadful wou'd appear,

While

While they their own ill-luck in war repeated,
His modefty ftill made him blufh, to hear
How often he had them defeated.

III.

Through his whole life, the part he bore
   Was wonderful and great,
And yet it fo appear'd in nothing more,
   Than in his private laft retreat ;
For 'tis a ftranger thing to find
One man of fuch a worthy mind,
   As can difmifs the power which he has got,
Than millions of the polls and braves ;
Thofe defpicable fools and knaves,
Who fuch a pudder make,
Through dulnefs and miftake,
   In feeking after pow'r, and get it not.

IV.

When all the nation he had won,
   And with expence of blood had bought,
   Store great enough he thought
Of glory and renown ;
He then his arms laid down,
   With juft as little pride
   As if he had been of his enemies fide,
Or one of them cou'd do that were undone:
   He neither wealth, nor places fought :
   He never for himfelf but others fought :
     He was content to know,
     (For he had found it fo)
That, when he pleas'd to conquer, he was able,
And left the fpoil and plunder to the rabble.

He

He might have been a King,
But that he underſtood
How much it was a meaner thing
To be unjuſtly great, than honourably good.
V.
This from the world did admiration draw
And from his friends, both love and awe,
Remembring what he did in fight before :
    And his foes lov'd him too,
    As they were bound to do,
  Becauſe he was reſolv'd to fight no more.
So bleſs'd by all he dy'd ; but far more bleſs'd
    were we,
If we were ſure to live, till we could ſee
A man as great in war, as juſt in peace as he.

TO HIS MISTRESS,

WHAT a dull fool was I,
To think ſo groſs a lye,
  As that I ever was in love before ?
I have, perhaps, known one or two
  With whom I was content to be,
  At that which they call keeping company ;
But after all that they could do,
  I ſtill could be with more :
Their abſence never made me ſhed a tear ;
  And I can truly ſwear,
That till my eyes firſt gaz'd on you,
  I ne'er beheld that thing I could adore,

                           A world

A world of things muſt curiouſly be ſought,
A world of things muſt be together brought
To make up charms which have the power to ⎫
    move,   ⎬
Through a diſcerning eye, true love ;   ⎭
That is a maſter-piece above
What only looks and ſhape can do,
There muſt be wit and judgment too ;
Greatneſs of thought and worth which draw
From the whole world, reſpeƈt and awe.
She that would raiſe a noble love, muſt find
Ways to beget a paſſion for her mind;
She muſt be that, which ſhe to be wou'd ſeem;
For all true love is grounded on eſteem :
Plainneſs and truth gain more a generous heart
Than all the crooked ſubtleties of art.
She muſt be---What ſaid I ? She muſt be you,
None but yourſelf that miracle can do;
At leaſt, I'm ſure, thus much I plainly ſee,
None but yourſelf e'er did it upon me :
'Tis you alone that can my heart ſubdue,
To you alone it always ſhall be true ;
Your god-like ſoul is that which rules my fate, ⎫
It does in me new paſſions ſtill create,   ⎬
For love of you all women elſe I hate :   ⎭
But oh ! your body too is ſo divine,
I kill myſelf with wiſhing you all mine.
In pain and anguiſh night and day,
I faint, and melt away :
In vain againſt my grief I ſtrive,
   My entertainment now is crying,
And all the ſenſe I have of being alive,
   Is that I feel myſelf a dying.

A DES-

A DESCRIPTION OF FORTUNE.

FORTUNE made up of toys, and impudence,
That common jade that has not common fenfe,
But fond of bufinefs, infolently dares
Pretend to rule, yet fpoils the world's affairs:
She's fluttering up and down, her favour throws ⎫
On the next met, not minding what fhe does, ⎬
Nor why, nor whom fhe helps, nor merit knows: ⎭
Sometimes fhe fmiles, then like a fury raves,
And feldom truly loves but fools and knaves.
Let her love whom fhe will, I fcorn to woo her;
While fhe ftays with me, I'll be civil to her;
But if fhe offers once to move her wings,
I'll fling her back all her vain gewgaw things;
And arm'd with virtue, will more glorious ftand,
Than if the bitch ftill bent at my command.
I'll marry honefty tho' ne'er fo poor;
Rather than follow fuch a dull blind whore.

UPON FELTON, THAT WAS HANGED IN CHAINS FOR THE MURDER OF THE DUKE OF BUCKINGHAM, IN THE REIGN OF KING CHARLES I.

HERE uninterr'd fufpends, tho' not to fave,
Surviving friends th' expences of a grave,
Felton's dead earth, which to the world will be
Its own fad monument; his eulogy,
As large as fame, which whether bad or good
I fay not, by himfelf 'twas wrote in blood;

For

For which his body is intomb'd in air,
Arch'd o'er with heav'n, fet with a thoufand fair
And glorious ftars, a noble fepulchre,
Which time itfelf can't ruinate, and where
Th' impartial worm (that is not brib'd to fpare
Princefs corrupt in marble) cannot fhare
His flefh, which oft the charitable fkies
Imbalm with tears, daining thofe obfequies,
So long to men fhall laft, 'till pitying fowl
Contend to reach his body to his foul.

A CONSOLATORY EPISTLE TO CAPTAIN JULIAN, THE MUSES NEWS-MONGER, IN HIS CONFINEMENT.

DEAR friend, when thofe we love are in di-
    ftrefs,
Kind verfe may comfort, tho' it can't redrefs;
Nor can I think fuch zeal you'll difcommend,
Since poetry has been fo much your friend:
On that thou'ft liv'd and flourifh'd all thy time;
Nay more, maintain'd a family by rhime;
And that's a mark that Dryden ne'er could hit,
He lives upon his penfion not his wit:
E'en gentle George (flux'd both in tongue and
    purfe)
Shunning one fnare, yet fell into a worfe.
A man may be reliev'd once in his life,
But who can be reliev'd that has a wife?
Otway can hardly guts from gaol preferve,
And, tho' he's very fat, he's like to ftarve:

And

And fing-fong Durfey (plac'd beneath abufes)
Lives by his impudence, and not the mufes:
Poor Crown too has his third days mix'd with gall,
He lives fo ill, he hardly lives at all.
Shadwell and Settle both with rhimes are fraught,
But can't between 'em mufter up a groat :
Nay, Lee in Bethl'em now fees better days,
Than when applauded for his bombaft plays ;
He knows no care, nor feels fharp want no more,
And that is what he ne'er could fay before :
Thus while our bards are famifh'd by their wit,
Thou who haft none at all, yet thriv'ft by it.
Were't poffible that wit could turn a penny,
Poets might then grow rich as well as any:
For 'tis not wit to have a great eftate,
The blind effect of fortune and of fate :
Since oft we fee a coxcomb dull and vain,
Brim-full of cafh, yet empty in his brain :
Nor is it wit that makes the lawyer prize
His dangl'd gown : 'tis knavery in difguife :
Nor is it wit that makes the tradefman great,
'Tis the compendious art to lye and cheat.
The bafe ftrumpet ftill may rant and rail,
'Tis not her wit fhe lives by, but her tail:
Nor is it wit that drills the ftatefman on
To wafte the fweets of life, fo quickly gone :
For 'tis not wit that brings a man to hanging,
That goes no farther than a harmlefs banging.
How juftly then doft thou our praife deferve,
That got'ft thy bread where all men elfe did ftarve ?
But what's more ftrange, the miracle was wrought
By one that ha'nt the leaft pretence to thought :

And

And he that had no meaning to do wrong,
Can't fuffer fure, for his no meaning, long.
And that's the confolation that I bring;
Thou art too dull, to think a treach'rous thing,
The thoughtful traytor 'tis offends the king.

A FAMILIAR EPISTLE TO MR. JULIAN,
SECRETARY TO THE MUSES.

THOU common-fhore of this poetic town,
Where all our excrements of wit are thrown.
For fonnet, fatyr, bawdry, blafphemy,
Are emptied and difburden'd all on thee:
The chol'rick wight, untruffing in a rage,
Finds thee, and leaves his load upon thy page.
Thou Julian, or thou wife Vefpafian rather,
Doft from this dung thy well pick'd guineas gather.
All mifchief's thine tranfcribing, thou wilt ftoop
From lofty Middlefex, to lowly Scroop:
What times are thefe, when in that hero's room,
Bow-bending Cupid does with ballads come,
And little Afhton offers to the bum----
Can two fuch pigmies fuch a weight fupport,
Two fuch Tom-Thumbs, of fatyr in a court?
Poor George grows old, his mufe is worn out of
        fafhion;
Hoarfly fhe fung Ephelia's lamentation.
Lefs art thou helpt by Dryden's bed-rid age,
That drone has left his fting upon the ftage.
Refolve me, poor apoftate, this one doubt,
What hope haft thou to rub this winter out?

2   Know

Know and be thankful then, for providence,
By me has fent thee this intelligence.
A knight there is, if thou can'ft gain his grace,
Known by the name of the Hard-favour'd face,
For prowefs of the pen, renown'd is he,
Defcended from Don Quixot lineally.
And though like him unfortunate he prove,
Undaunted in attempts of wit and love.
Of his unfinifh'd face, what fhall I fay,
But that 'twas made of Adam's own red clay,
That much, much oak was on it beftow'd,
God's image 'tis not, but fome Indian god.
Our chriftian earth can no refemblance bring,
But ware of Portugal for fuch a thing.
Such carbuncles his fiery face confefs,
As no Hungarian water can redrefs.
A face which fhou'd he fee, but heaven was kind,
And to indulge his felf-love, made him blind.
He dares not ftir abroad for fear to meet,
Curfes of teeming women in the ftreet.
The leaft cou'd happen from that hideous fight ⎤
Is that they fhou'd mifcarry with the fright : ⎬
Heaven guard 'em from the likenefs of the ⎭
    knight.
Such is our charming Strephon's outward man
His inward parts let thofe defcribe who can :
But by his monthly flowers difcharg'd abroad,
'Till full, brim full of paftoral and ode:
E'er while he honour'd Bertha with his flame ;
And now he chants no lefs Lovifa's name.
For when his paffion has been babling long,
The froth at laft breaks into a fong.

                                     But

But fure no mortal creature at one time,
Was e'er fo far o'er gone with love and rhime.
To his dear felf of poetry he talks,
His hands and feet are fcanning as he walks.
His fqueezing looks, his pangs of wit accufe,
The very fymptoms of a breeding mufe.
And all to gain the great Lovifa's grace,
But never wit did pimp for fuch a face.
There's not a nymph in city, town or court,
But Strephon's billet doux's have made them fport.
Still he loves on, yet ftill as fure to mifs,
As they, that wafh an Ethiope's face, or his.
What fate unlucky Strephon does attend,
Never to get a miftrefs, or a friend ?
Strephon a like both wits and fools deteft,
Becaufe, like Æfop's bat, half bird half beaft.
For fools to poetry have no pretence,
And common wit fuppofes common fenfe.
Not quite fo low as fool, nor quite a top,
But hangs between 'em both, and is a fop.
His morals, like his wit, are motley too ;
He keeps from arrant knave with much ado.
But vanity and lying fo prevail,
That one grain more of each wou'd turn the fcale.
He wou'd be more a villain had he time,
But he's fo wholly taken up with rhime,
That he miftakes his talent, all his care
Is to be thought a poet fine and fair.
Small-beer and gruel are his meat and drink,
The diet he prefcribes himfelf to think.
Rhime next his heart, he takes at morning-peep,
Some love-epiftles at his hours of fleep.

So

So between elegy and ode we fee,
Strephon is in a courfe of poetry.
  This is the man ordain'd to do thee good,
The Pelican to feed thee with his blood.
Thy wit, thy poet, nay thy friend, for he,
Is fit to be a friend to none but thee:
Make fure of him, and of his mufe betimes,
For all his ftudy is hung round with rhimes.
Laugh at him, juftle him, yet ftill he writes,
In rhime he challenges, in rhime he fights.
Charg'd with the laft and bafeft infamy,
His bufinefs is to think what rhimes to lie:
Which found, in fury he retorts again,
Strephon's a very dragon at his pen.
His brother murder'd, and his mother whor'd,
His miftrefs loft, and yet his pen's his fword.

THE LOST MISTRESS. A COMPLAINT
AGAINST THE COUNTESS OF -------.*

FORSAKEN Strephon, in a lonefome glade,
By nature for defpairing forrows made,
Beneath a blafted oak had laid him down,
By light'ning that, as he by love o'er thrown.
Upon the moffy root he lean'd his head,
While at his feet a murmuring current led

* Probably the countefs of Shrewfbury, whofe lord he
killed in a duel on her account, and who is faid to have
held the duke's horfe, difguifed like a page, during the combat; to reward his prowefs in which, fhe went to bed in the
fhirt ftained with her hufband's blood. The loves of this
tender pair are recorded by Pope.
    Gallant and gay, in Cliveden's proud alcove,
    The bow'r of wanton Shrewfbury and love.

Her ſtreams, that ſympathiz'd with his ſad moans,
The neighb'ring echoes anſwer'd all his groans.
Then as the dewy morn reſtor'd the day,
Whilſt ſtretch'd on earth the ſilent mourner lay;
At laſt into theſe doleful ſounds he broke,
Obdurate rocks diſſolving whilſt he ſpoke;
What language can my injur'd paſſion frame,
That knows not how to give its wrongs a name;
My ſuff'ring heart can all relief refuſe,
Rather than her, it did adore, accuſe.
Teach me, ye groves, ſome art to eaſe my pain, ⎱
Some ſoft reſentments that may leave no ſtain ⎰
On her lov'd name, and then I will complain. ⎰
Till then, to all my wrongs I will be blind,
And whilſt ſhe's cruel, call her but unkind.
As all my thoughts to pleaſe her were employ'd,
When of her ſmiles the bleſſing I enjoy'd,
So now by her forſaken and forlorn,
I'll rack invention to excuſe her ſcorn.
While ſhe to truth and me unjuſt does prove,
From her to fate the blame I will remove;
Say, 'twas a deſtiny ſhe cou'd not ſhun,
Fate made her change that I might be undone.
E'er with perfidious guilt her ſoul I'll tax,
I'll charge it on the frailty of her ſex,
Doom'd her firſt mother's error to purſue:
She ne'er was falſe, cou'd woman have been true.
Let all her ſex henceforth be ever ſo. ⎱
She had the power to make my bliſs or woe, ⎰
And ſhe has given my heart its mortal blow. ⎰
In love the bleſſing of my life I clos'd,
And in her cuſtody that love diſpos'd.
In one dear freight all's loſt! of her bereft,
I have no hope, no ſecond comfort left.

If

If fuch another beauty I could find,
A beauty too that bore a conftant mind,
Ev'n that could bring me medicine for my pain,
I lov'd not at a rate to love again.
No change can eafe for my fick heart prepare,
Widow'd to hope, and wedded to defpair.
  Thus figh'd the fwain, at length his o'er-
        watch'd eyes
A foft beguiling flumber did furprize;
Whofe flatt'ring comfort prov'd both fhort and vain,
Refrefh'd, like flaves from racks, to greater pain.

UPON NOTHING. A POEM.

BY THE D. OF B. AND THE E. OF ROCHESTER.

NOTHING, thou elder-brother, even to fhade,
Who hadft a being ere the world was made,
And well fixt alone, of ending not afraid.

Ere time and place were, time and place were not,
When primitive nothing, fomething ftrait begat;
Then all proceeded from the great united what!

Something, the general attribute of all,
Sever'd from thee its fole original.
Into thy boundlefs felf, muft undiftinguifh'd fall.

Yet fomething did thy nothing power command,
And from thy fruitful emptineffes hand,
Snatch men, beafts, birds, fire, water, air and land.

Matter, the wicked'ft offspring of thy race,
By form affifted, fled from thy embrace,
And rebel light, obfcur'd thy rev'rend dufky face.
                L 2   With

With form and matter, time and place did join ;
Body, thy foe, with thefe did leagues combine,
To fpoil thy peaceful reign, and ruin all thy line.

But turn-coat time, affifts the foe amain,
And brib'd by thee, deftroys their fhort-liv'd reign,
And to thy hungry womb, drives back thy flaves
       again.

Thy myfteries are hid from Laick eyes,
And the Divine alone by warrant pries
Into thy bofom, where the truth in private lies.

Yet this of thee, the wife may truly fay,
Thou from the virtuous, nothing take'ft away,
And to be part of thee, the wicked wifely pray.

Great negative! how vainly would the wife
Enquire, defign, diftinguifh, teach, devife,
Did'ft not thou ftand to point their blind philofo-
       phies.

Is, or is not, the two great ends of fate,
Of true or falfe, the fubject of debate,
That perfects or deftroys defigns of ftate.

When they have rack'd the politicians breaft,
Within thy bofom moft fecurely reft,
Reduc'd to thee are leaft, tho' fafe and beft.

But nothing, why doth fomething ftill permit,
That facred monarchs fhould at council fit
With perfons thought, at beft, for nothing fit?

Whilft weighty fomething, modeftly abftains
From princes courts, and from our ftatefmens
       brains ;
And nothing there like ftately nothing reigns.

Nothing,

Nothing, that dwells with fools, in grave difguife,
For whom they rev'rend forms and fhapes devife,
Lawn fleeves, furs, gowns, when they like thee
  look wife.

French truth, Dutch prowefs, Britifh policy,
Hybernian learning, Scots fidelity,
Spaniards difpatch, Danes wit are mainly feen in
  thee.

The great man's gratitude to his beft friend,
Kings promifes, whores vows, tow'rds thee bend,
Flow fwiftly into thee, and in thee ever end.

A TRIAL OF THE POETS FOR THE BAYES. IN IMITATION OF A SATYR IN BOILEAU. BY THE SAME.

SINCE the fons of the Mufes grew num'rous
  and loud,
For th' appeafing fo factious, and clam'rous a
  croud,
Apollo thought fit, in fo weighty a caufe,
T' eftablifh a government, leader, and laws.
The hopes of the bayes, at the fummoning call,
Had drawn them together, the Devil and all ;
All thronging and lift'ning, they gap'd for the
  blefling :
No prefbyter fermon had more crouding and pref-
  fing :
In the head of the gang, John Dryden appear'd,
That ancient grave wit fo long lov'd and fear'd,

         But

But Apollo had heard a ftory in town,
Of his quitting the Mufes, to wear the black
  gown;
And fo gave him leave now his poetry's done,
To let him turn prieft fince R---- is turn'd nun.
This reverend author was no fooner fet by,
But Apollo had got gentle George * in his eye.
And frankly confeft, of all men that writ,
There's none had more fancy, fenfe, judgment
  and wit?
But in th' crying fin, idlenefs, he was fo harden'd,
That his long feven year's filence, was not to be
  pardon'd.
----W----y † was the next man fhew'd his face,
But Apollo e'en thought him too good for the
  place;
No gentleman writer that office fhould bear,
But a trader in wit the laurel fhould wear,
As none but a Cit---e'er makes a Lord-Mayor.
Next into the croud, Tom Shadwell does wallow,
And fwears by his guts, his paunch, and his tallow,
That 'tis he alone beft pleafes the age,
Himfelf, and his wife, have fupported the ftage:
Apollo well pleas'd with fo bonny a lad,
T' oblige him, he told him, he fhould be huge
  glad,
Had he half fo much wit, as he fancy'd he had.
Nat. Lee ftept in next, in hopes of a prize,
Apollo remember'd he had hit once in thrice;
By the rubies in's face, he could not deny,
But he had as much wit as wine could fupply;

* Sir George Etheredge.   † Mr. Wycherly.

Confeft

Confeft that indeed he had a mufical note,
But fometimes ftrain'd fo hard that he rattled in
    throat ;
Yet owning he had fenfe, t'encourage him for't,
He made him his Ovid in Auguftus's court.
Poor Settle, his trial was the next came about,
He brought him an Ibrahim with the preface torn
    out,
And humbly defir'd he might give no offence ;
Dam him, cries Shadwell, he cannot write fenfe :
And Bancks, cry'd Newport, I hate that dull
    rogue ;
Apollo confidering he was not in vogue,
Would not truft his dear Bays with fo modeft a
    fool,
And bid the great boy be fent back to fchool.
Tom Otway came next, Tom Shadwell's dear
    Zany,
And fwears, for heroicks, he writes beft of any :
Don Carlos his pockets fo amply had fill'd,
That his mange was quite cur'd, and his lice were
    all kill'd ;
Anababaluthu put in for a fhare,
And little Tom Effences author was there :
But Apollo had feen his face on the ftage,
And prudently did not think fit to engage,
The fcum of a play-houfe, for the prop of an
    age.
In the numerous croud that incompafs'd him
    round,
Little ftarch'd Johnny Crown at his elbow he found,

His cravat-ftring new iron'd, he gently did ftretch
His lily white hand out, the laurel to reach.
Alledging that he had moft right to the Bays,
For writing romances, and fh-ting of plays:
Apollo rofe up, and gravely confeft,
Of all men that writ, his talent was beft;
For fince pain and difhonour mans life only damn,⎫
The greateft felicity mankind can claim,   ⎪
Is to want fenfe of fmart, and to be paft fenfe   ⎬
   of fhame;   ⎭
And to perfect his blifs in poetical rapture,
He bid him be dull to the end of the chapter.
The poetefs Afra, next fhew'd her fweet face,
And fwore by her poetry, and her black ace.
The laurel by a double right was her own,
For the plays fhe had writ, and the conquefts fhe
   had won.
Apollo acknowledg'd 'twas hard to deny her,
Yet to deal frankly and ingenuoufly by her,
He told her were conquefts, and charms her pre-
   tence,
She ought to have pleaded a dozen years fince.
Nor could Durfy forbear for the laurel to ftickle,⎫
Protefting that he had the honour to tickle   ⎬
Th' ears of the town, with his dear madam   ⎪
   Fickle.   ⎭
With other pretenders, whofe names I'd rehearfe,
But that they're too long to ftand in my verfe:
Apollo quite tir'd with their tedious harangue, ⎫
At laft found Tom Betterton's face in the gang; ⎬
For fince poets without the kind players may   ⎪
   hang,   ⎭

                                   By

By his one facred light he folemnly fwore,
That in fearch of a laureat, he'd look out no
      more.
A general murmur ran quite thro' the hall,
To think that the Bays to an actor fhould fall;
Tom told e'm, to put his defert to the teft,
That he had MAID plays as well as the beft,
And was the great'ft wonder the age ever bore,
Of all the play-fcriblers that e'er writ before,
His wit had moft worth, and modefty in't,
For he had writ plays, yet ne'er came in print.

A SATYR UPON THE FOLLIES OF THE MEN OF THE AGE. BY THE SAME.

WHEN Shakefpear, Johnfon, Fletcher, rul'd
      the ftage,
They took fo bold a freedom with the age,
That there was fcarce a knave, or fool in town
Of any note, but had his picture fhown;
And (without doubt) tho' fome it may offend, ⎫
Nothing helps more than fatyr, to amend ⎬
Ill-manners, or is trulier virtue's friend: ⎭
Princes may laws ordain, priefts gravely preach,
But poets more fuccefsfully will teach;
For as a paffing-bell frights from his meat,
The greedy fick-man, that too much would eat;
So when a vice ridiculous is made,
Our neighbours fhame keeps us from growing bad,
But wholefome remedies few palates pleafe,
Men rather love what flatters their difeafe;
                              Pimps,

Pimps, parafites, buffoons, and all the crew
That under friendfhip's name weak man undo,
Find their falfe fervice kindlier underftood,
Than fuch as tell both truths to do us good;
Look where you will, and you fhall hardly find
A man without fome ficknefs of the mind:
In vain we wife would feem, while ev'ry luft
Whifks us about, as whirl-winds do the duft.
Here for fome needlefs gain, the wretch is hurl'd
From pole to pole, and flav'd about the world,
While the reward of all his pains and care,
Ends in that defpicable thing, his heir.
There a vain fop mortgages all his land,
To buy that gawdy play-thing, a command;
To ride a cock-horfe, wear a fcarf at's arfe,
And play the pudding in a May-day farce;
Here one whom God to make a fool thought fit,
In fpite of Providence will be a wit;
But wanting ftrength t'uphold his ill made choice,
Sets up with lewdnefs, blafphemy and noife;
There at his miftrefs' feet a lover lies,
And for a tawdry painted baby dies;
Falls on his knees, adores; and is afraid
Of the vain idol he himfelf has made:
Thefe, and a thoufand fools unmention'd here,
Hate poets all, becaufe they poets fear;
Take heed (they cry) yonder mad dog will bite,
He cares not whom he falls on in his fit;
Come but in's way and ftrait a new lampoon
Shall fpread your mangled fame about the town.
But why am I this Bug-bear to you all?
My pen is dip'd in no fuch bitter gall.

                                        " He

" He that can rail at one he calls his friend,
" Or hear him (abfent) wrong'd, and not defend;
" Who for the fake of fome ill-natur'd jefts,
" Tells what he fhould conceal, invents the reft;
" To fatal mid-night quarrels can betray,   ..
" His brave companion, and then run away;
" Leaving him to be murder'd in the ftreet,
" Then put it off with fome buffoon conceit;
" This, this is he you fhould beware of all,
" Yet him a pleafant, witty man, you call;"
To whet your dull debauches up and down,
You feek him as top fidler of the town:
But if I laugh when the court-coxcombs fhow
To fee the booby Sotus dance provoe;
Or chattering Porus from the fide-box grin,
Trick like a lady's monkey new made clean:
To me the name of Railer ftraight you give,
Call me a man that knows not how to live.
   But wenches to their keepers true fhall turn,
Stale maids of honour proffer'd hufbands fcorn,
Great ftatefmen flattery and clinches hate,
And long in office, die without eftate;
Againft a bribe, court-judges fhall decide,
The city knavery want, the clergy pride:
E'er that black malice in my rhimes you find,
That wrongs a worthy man, or hurts a friend.
But then perhaps you'll fay, Why do you write,
What you think harmlefs mirth, the world thinks
      fpight.
Why fhould your fingers itch to have a lafh
At Simius the buffoon, or cully Bafh?
What is't to you, if Alidore's fine whore,
Lies with fome fop, whilft he's fhut out of door:
                          Confider

Confider pray, that dang'rous weapon, wit,
Frightens a million, when a few you hit:
Whip but a cur, as you ride thro' a town,
And ftrait his fellow curs the quarrel own,
Each knave, or fool that's confcious of a crime,
Tho' he 'fcapes now, looks for't another time.
   Sir, I confefs all you have faid is true,
But who has not fome folly to purfue?
Milo turn'd Quixot, fancy'd battles, fights,
When the fifth bottle had encreas'd the lights,
War, like dirt pies, our hero Paris forms,
Which defperate Beffus without armour ftorms.
Cormus, the kindeft hufband e'er was born,
Still courts the fpark that does his brows adorn;
Invites him home to dine, and fills his veins
With the hot blood which his dear Doxy drains.
   Grandio thinks himfelf a beau Garçon,
Goggles his eyes, writes letters up and down,
And with his faucy love plagues all the town;
While pleas'd to have his vanity thus fed,
He's caught with C---- that old hag, a bed.
But fhou'd I all the crying follies tell,
That roufe the fleeping fatyr from his cell,
I to my reader fhou'd as tedious prove,
As that old fpark, Albanus, making love:
Or florid Rofcius, when with fome fmooth flam,
He gravely on the publick ftrives to fham.
   Hold then, my mufe, 'tis time to make an end,
Leaft taxing others, thou thyfelf offend.
The world's a wood, in which all lofe their way,
Though by a different path each goes aftray.

TIMON,

TIMON, A SATYR, IN IMITATION OF MONSIEUR BOILEAU, UPON SEVERAL PASSAGES IN SOME NEW PLAYS THEN ACTED UPON THE STAGE.

A. *WHAT*, Timon, *does old age begin to approach.*
That thus thou droop'ſt under a night's debauch ?
Haſt thou loſt deep to needy rogues *on tick,*
Who ne'er could pay, and muſt be paid next week?
 Timon. Neither, alas ! but, a dull dining ſot
Seiz'd me i'th' Mall, who juſt my name had got ;
He runs upon me, cries, dear rogue, I'm thine,
With me ſome wits of my acquaintance dine.
I tell him I'm engaged ; but as a whore,
With modeſty, enſlaves her ſpark the more ;
The longer I deny'd, the more he preſt,
At laſt I e'en conſent to be his gueſt ;
He takes me in his coach, and as we go,
Pulls out a libel of a ſheet or two ;
Inſipid as the praiſe of pious queens,
Or Shadwell's unaſſiſted former ſcenes ;
Which he admir'd, and prais'd at every line ;
At laſt it was ſo ſharp it muſt be mine :
I vow'd I was no more a wit than he,
Unpractis'd, and unbleſt in poetry :
A ſong to Phillis I perhaps might make,
And never rhim'd, but for my miſtreſs' ſake :
I envy'd no man's fortune, nor his fame,
Nor ever thought of a revenge ſo tame.
He knew my ſtile, he ſwore, it was in vain,
Thus to deny the iſſue of my brain.

Chok'd

Chok'd with his flattery, I no anfwer make,
But filent leave him to his dear miftake.
Of a well-meaning fool I'm moft afraid,
Who fillily repeats what was well faid.
But this is not the worft, when he came home,
He afk'd, are Sedley, Buckhurft, Savil come?
No. but there were above Halfwit and Huff,
Kickum, and Dingboy. Oh! that's well enough;
They're all brave fellows, cries mine hoft, lets
        dine,
I long to have my belly full of wine.
They'll fmartly write, and fight, I dare affure you,
They're men I'faith; *Tam Marte quam Mecurio.*
I faw my error, but 'twas then too late,
No means, nor hopes appear'd for a retreat:
Well, we falute, and each man takes his feat.
Boy, cries my fot, is my wife ready yet?
A wife, good Gods! a fop, and bullies too!
For one poor meal, what muft I undergo?
In comes my lady ftrait, fhe had been fair,
Fit to give love, and to prevent defpair;
But age, beauty's incurable difeafe,
Had left her more defire, than power to pleafe.
As cocks will ftrive although their fpurs be gone,
She with her one bleer eye to fmite began;
Tho' nothing elfe, fhe (in defpight of time)
Preferv'd the affectation of her prime:
However you begun, fhe brought in love,
And hardly from that fubject would remove:
We chanc'd to fpeak of the French king's fuccefs,
My lady wonder'd much how heaven could blefs
A man that lov'd two women at one time;
But·more, how he to them excus'd his crime.
                                        She

She aſked Huff, If love's flame he e'er felt !
He anſwer'd bluntly do you think I'm gelt ?
She at his plainneſs ſmil'd, then turn'd to me,
Love in young minds precedes ev'n poetry ;
You to that paſſion can no ſtranger be,
But wits are given to inconſtancy.
She had run on I think till now, but meat
Came up, and ſuddenly ſhe took her ſeat :
I thought the dinner would make ſome amends,
When my good hoſt cry'd out, " You're all my
    " friends :
" Our own plain fare, and the beſt terſe the bull
" Affords, I give you, and your bellies full ;
" As for French kick-ſhaws, cellery, and champain,
" Ragous and fricaſſes, in troth we'ave none :"
Here's a good dinner toward, thought I, when
    ſtrait,
Up came a piece of beef, full horſe-man weight ;
Hard as the arſe of M——, under which
The coachman ſweats, as ridden by a witch ;
A diſh of carrots, each of 'em as long
As T——l that to fair counteſs did belong ;
Which her ſmall pillow could not ſo well hide,
But viſiters his flaming head eſpy'd :
Pig, gooſe, and capon follow'd in the rear,
With all that country bumkins call good cheer :
Serv'd up with ſauces all of eighty-eight,
When our tough youth, wreſtled, and threw the
    weight :
And now the bottle briſkly flies about,
Inſtead of ice, wrapt up in a wet clout :
A brimmer follows, the third bit we eat,
Small beer becomes our drink, and wine our meat :
    The

The table was fo large, that in lefs fpace,
A man might fix old fage Italians place:
Each man had as much room as porter B——
Or Harris had in Cullen's bufhel ——
And now the wine began to work, mine hoft ⎱
Had been a colonel, we muft hear him boaft, ⎰
Not of towns won but an eftate he loft
For the king's fervice, which indeed he fpent, ⎱
Whoring and drinking but with good intent; ⎰
He talkt much of a plot and money lent
In Cromwell's time: As for my lady fhe
Complain'd our love was coarfe, our poetry
Unfit for modeft ears, fmall whores, and play'rs,
Were of our hair-brain'd youth the only cares;
Who were too wild for any virtuous league,
Too rotten to confummate the intrigue.
Falkland fhe prais'd, and Suckling's eafy pen,
And feem'd to tafte their former parts again.
Mine hoft drinks to the beft in Chriftendom,
And decently my lady quits the room.
Left to ourfelves, of feveral things we prate,
Some regulate the ftage, and fome the ftate:
Halfwit, cries up my lord of Orréry,
Ah! how well Muftapha, and Zanger die;
His fenfe is fo little forc'd that by one line
You may the other eafily divine:
And which is worfe, if any worfe can be,
He never faid one word of it to me.
There's lufcious poetry! you'd fwear 'twas profe;
So little on the fenfe the rhimes impofe:
D--m me (fays Dingboy) in my mind G-df--ns, ⎱
Etheridge write airy fongs, and foft lampoons, ⎰
The beft of any man; as for your nouns,
                                        Grammar,

Grammar, and rules of art, he knows 'em not,
Yet writ two taking plays, without one plot.
Huff, was for Settle, and Morocco prais'd,
Said rumbling words, like drums, his courage
    rais'd;
Whofe broad built bulks the boiſt'rous billows bear.
Zaphee, and Sally, Mugadore, Oran,
The fam'd Arzile, Alcazer, Tituan ;
Was ever braver language writ by man ?
Kickum for Crown declar'd, ſaid in romance,
He had outdone the very wits of France :
Witneſs Pandion ; and his Charles the Eight,
Where a young monarch, careleſs of his fate,
Tho' foreign troops, and rebels ſhook his ſtate ;
Complains another ſight afflicts him more,
(*Viz.*) The Queen's galleys rowing from the ſhore,
Fitting their oars, and tacking to be gone,
Whilſt ſporting waves ſmil'd on the riſing ſun.
Waves ſmiling on the ſun ! I am ſure that's new,
And, 'twas well thought on, give the Devil his due.
My Hoſt, who had ſaid nothing in an hour,
Roſe up, and prais'd the Indian Emperor ;
As if our old world modeſtly withdrew,
And here, in private, had brought forth anew.
Theſe are two lines, who but he durſt preſume
To make th' old world a new withdrawing room?
Whereof another world ſhe's brought to bed ;
What a brave midwife is a laureat's head !

    But pox upon theſe ſcriblers, what d'ye think,
Will Zouches this year any champain drink ?
Will Turene fight him? Without doubt, ſays Huff,
If they two meet their meeting will be rough,

D—mn me (fays Dingboy) the French cowards are,
They pay, but th' Englifh, Scots, and Switz
        make war:
In gawdy troops, at a review they fhine,
But dare not with the Germans battle join:
What now appears like courage, is not fo,
'Tis a fhort pride which from fuccefs does grow.
On their firft blow, they'll fhrink into thofe fears
They fhew'd at Creffy, Agin-Court, Poictiers;
Their lofs was infamous, honour fo ftain'd
Is by a nation not to be regain'd.
What they were then, I know not, now they're
        brave,
He that deneies it, lies, and is a flave
(Says Huff, and frown'd;) fays Dingboy, that
        do I;
And at that word, at t'others head let fly
A greafy Plate, when fuddenly they all
Together by the ears in parties fall:
Halfwit with Dingboy joins, Kickum with Huff, ⎫
Their fwords were fafe, and fo we let 'em cuff, ⎬
Till, they, my Hoft, and I, had all enough. ⎭
Their rage once over they begin to treat,
And fix frefh bottles muft the peace compleat;
I ran down ftairs, with a vow ne'er more,
To drink beer-glaffes, and hear Hectors roar,

ADVICE

ADVICE TO A PAINTER, TO DRAW MY L. A——TON; GRAND MINISTER OF STATE.

FIRST draw an arrant fop, from top to toe,
Whofe very looks at firſt daſh ſhew him ſo :
Give him a mean proud garb, a dapper face,
A pert dull grin, a black-patch crofs his face,
Two goggle-eyes, ſo clear; tho' very dead,
That one may ſee, thro' them, quite thro' his head.
Let every nod of his, and ſubtile wink,
Declare the fool would talk, but cannot think.
Let him all other fools ſo far ſurpaſs,
That fools themſelves point at him for an aſs.
    Next all his implements of folly draw.
His iv'ry-ſtaff, his ſnuff-box and * TATTA,
That pretty babe that makes his lordſhip glad;
And all the company beſides ſo ſad ;
She who in ſtate is brought, to ſmooth his brow,
When he has rul'd the roaſt, the Lord knows how.
For tho' to us he's ſtately like a king,
He'll joke and droll with her like any thing.
    Paint at the door, attending night and noon,
Povey the wit, and R--- the beau Garçon,
Who at his entering ſhews a foot of chin,
To let you know his face is coming in :
Behind him let advance, in fear and choller,
Tit----s the Jew, the pedant, and no ſcholar.
Who for bold ſilly jeſts, is ſo renown'd ;
Then ſhut the door, and let 'em all clinch round,
For that's their proper talent; tho' our fate
Has made them woeful miniſters of ſtate.

* His Daughter.

M 2   UPON

UPON THE INSTALMENT OF SIR THOMAS OS----N, AND THE LATE DUKE OF NEWCASTLE.

ALL who had hopes it e'er might be their fate,
To have preferment in the church or ftate,
At Windfor were commanded to appear,
To fee an object ftrange, was fhewing there.
Coach-fulls of fools went thither great and fmall;
Five lords, fix bifhops, and the B---es all:
Backwell and Vyner, with the merry crew,
Of all the bankers, and the voters too;
Befides a throng of ladies, that did prefs
To pay their duty to the treafurefs:
Who, tho' my lord, to govern things may boaft,
Does with her honour's prudence rule the roaft,
Both he, and fhe, are perfons of fine parts,
And have peculiar ways of gaining hearts.
Firft he brings always with him a fweet favour;
To win the courtier's love, and courtier's favour;
Then fhe puts on a fore-head-cloath to pleafe
The city and the godly folk, fhe fays:
And fo with eafe, and without coft, or pother,
They get a world of friends one way, or other.
For they were worfe than devils, could oppofe
Such taking charms, both of the eyes and nofe.
Each writer there, was fitted for his ftation
Babb's for deep fenfe, Trerice for converfation,
And Lauderdale to gratify the nation.
Progers did reprefent iniquity.
And that old cuckold F---it you might fee
Kifling's fore-finger for civility.

And

And whiftling gravely to himfelf a fong,
He has been practifing, God knows how long!
This being adjufted, on they all did prance,
Throwing their arms out *a-la-mode de France:*
Which made men ftare, and put them to a ftand,
Every one crying by my troth, 'tis grand ;
St. George himfelf came in upon this fummons,
Dreft like a member of the houfe of commons ;
With a plain fuit, plain belt, plain band and ftaff,
And ready ftill from looking grave, to laugh,
For thefe brave houfe of commons men we fee,
Do all both Polls and Drolls affect to be.
More to refemble them, his look was proud, ⎫
His gate fantaftick; and he afk'd aloud   ⎬
Of all he met with, what means all this croud ? ⎭
One of the ftanders by reply'd----they fay,
Two pale knights are to be inftall'd to-day.
Strait Albemarle advanc'd with Lauderdale,
Methinks then, quoth St. *George,* thefe are not
      pale ;
They look as if they had been taking bumpers,
Yes faid the other, thefe two knights are thumpers.
Who for their bulk were chofe, with much ado,
To grace the thinnefs of the other two.
Well, cries St. George, let's fee then who comes
      next ?
It was New-Caftle, who was much perplext,
Between the care of decently conveying,
And how to fave half of his offering.
The brave St. George ftrait knew he was an afs,
Yet for his father's fake, he let him pafs.

M 3   But

But whifper'd thus in pale Sir Of--n ear,
Away thou worthlefs rogue, what mak'ft thou here?
How dare you in this chapel keep a quarter,
With your blue lips, bluer than robes or garter?
Go, get a fhroud to match your face and breath,
Be dreft, as well as look and fmell, like death.
'Twas that alone at firft which nature meant,
Your loathfome carcafs ftill fhould reprefent,
For fo unlively, and fo naufeous too,
Is every thing you either fay or do;
That even your bafe ingratitude does give,
The leaft offenfive tokens, that you live.
You're fuch a fcurvy, ftinking, errant knight,
That when you fpeak, a man wou'd fwear you fh--;
Then in a trice he flew from thence and tore
His pert wife's croflet off; who curft and fwore,
Bit her thin lips, and railed like any punk,
Whilft pale Sir Of--n opened his — and ftunk.

UPON THE MONUMENT,

H ERE ftand I,
The Lord knows why,
But if I fall,
Have at you all.

UPON

UPON THE FOLLOWING PASSAGES
IN THE CONQUEST OF GRANADA,

A TRAGEDY WRITTEN BY MR. DRYDEN.

FO R as old Selin *was not mov'd by thee*
Neither will I by Selin's *daughter be.*
  A pie, a pudding, a pudding a pie,
A pie for me, and a pudding for thee:
A pudding for me, and a pie for thee,
And a pudding-pie for thee and me.

A NOTION TAKEN OUT OF TULLY'S
DIALOGUE, DE SENECTUTE.

IF all the Gods fhould now a fancy take, · -
Some one of us a raw young blade to make;
Is there a flave, or lord, (for lords we fee,
Nothing elfe now a-days, but flaves will be)
That wou'd not fay, Gods! in your doom be fteady.
I have been long enough a fool already.
Name but one feat of theirs fo little vain,
We fhould not blufh to practife o'er again.
They are fuch beaftly rogues in all they do,
Their very vices are unmanly too.
Wou'd you be dully drunk ? break open doors,
To kick a nafty bawd, or cuff poor whores ?
Or all we meet with in the ftreets abufe,
As our brave anti-wits and great ones ufe ?
Nay cou'd we yet do grander things than thefe,
Murther an harmlefs watchman on his knees;

Go

Go travel afterwards for more renown,
Come home again, cut capers up and down,
And then take Maſtricht, hard by Windſor Town.
Were not the worſt of death's a greater blifs,
'Than ſuch a vile, inſipid life as this?
    There never was but one, yet ſot enough
    Cou'd wiſh to live for ſuch baſe ſilly ſtuff.

THE PUMP-PARLIAMENT. A SATYR.

I.

Curse on such repreſentatives
That tell us all, our bairns and wives,
    Quoth Dick, with indignation;
They're but an engine to raiſe tax,
And the whole buſineſs of their acts,
    Is to undo the nation.

II.

Juſt like our rotten pump at home,
We pour in water when 'twon't come,
    And that way get more out;
So when mine Hoſt does money lack,
He money gives among this pack,
    And then it runs full ſpout.

III.

By wiſe folk I have oft been told,
Parl'ments grow nought as they grow old.
    We groan'd under the rump,
But ſure this is a heavier curſe,
'That ſucks and drains thus every purſe,
    By this old Whitehall pump.

OPTIMUM

OPTIMUM QUOD EVENIT·

OR, AN EPIGRAM OCCASIONED BY THE KING'S
REPROACHING HIM WITH AN OVERSIGHT.

B Y hidden fprings man's fmalleft actions move,
Wound up by an unerring hand above,
Why fay you then, that this or that's amifs;
Since nothing cou'd be better than what is?

THE CABIN-BOY.

N AY he could fail a yacht both nigh and large,
Knew how to trim a boat, and fteer a barge:
Cou'd fay his compafs, to the nation's joy,
And fwear as well as any cabin-boy.
But not one leffon of the ruling art,
Cou'd this dull blockhead ever get by heart.
Look over all the univerfal frame,
There's not a thing the will of man can name,
In which this ugly, perjur'd rogue delights,
But Ducks, and loit'ring, butter'd buns, and Whites.

THE DUCKS.

W HILST in the ftate all things look fmooth
    and fair,
I'll dabble up and down, and take the air.
But at the firft appearance of foul weather,
I and my ducks will quack away together.

VERSES

VERSES ON THE FOLLOWING TWO LINES OF MR. EDWARD HOWARD.

But Fame had fent forth all her nimble fpies,
To blaze this match, and lend to Fate fome eyes.

BUT wherefore all this pother about fame?
A man might fay, fays one: the very fame
Demand might well be made, another cries,
Of Fate; and how it got, from Fame, fuch eyes?
'Tis well; you're witty perfons both, fay I;
Yet to your wit this boldly I'll reply:
Fate is the twin of Chance, by which you find
Fate muft needs fee, except that Chance were
   blind:
For, among friends, 'twere inequality
To think one fhou'd be blind, and t'other fee.
Now tell me, criticks, do not all the wife
Profefs that which they fee, they fee with eyes?
And the fame figure do not I advance,
When I proteft, I faw a thing by chance?
Since then fo various things by chance we fee,
Fate might have eyes to multiplicity;
But our mild author fays, it has but fome;
'Thus, critick vile, thus I have ftruck thee dumb:
And thus fubfcribe myfelf, with heart, and hand,
The author's friend, moft humble fervant, and
       BUCKINGHAM.

A CON-

A

CONFERENCE

BETWEEN

His Grace, GEORGE late Duke of BUCKINGHAM, and father FITZGERALD, an Irish priest, whom King JAMES II. sent to his Grace in his sickness, to endeavour to pervert him to the popish persuasion.

FAITHFULLY TAKEN BY HIS SECRETARY.

Priest. MAY it please your grace, I come from his majesty, who sent me on purpose to wait on you.

Duke. I am exceedingly beholden to his majesty for all his favours. I thought I had long ago been out of his remembrance. Pray, Sir, take a chair. And what may your errand be?

Priest. His majesty being informed of your grace's illness, and, as it becomes a prince who has a true regard for his subjects, compassionating the dangerous circumstances you are in at present, commanded me to use my best endeavours to reclaim your grace from that heretical communion, 'tis now your unhappiness to embrace, and reconcile you to the catholick church, out of which there is no salvation.

Duke.

Duke. 1 perceive, Sir, you're a prieſt. S---am, bring up a bottle of wine, and clean glaſſes----do you ſmoke, Sir ?

Prieſt. An't pleaſe your grace, I did not come to drink, but---

Duke. Well, well, a glaſs now and then won't ſpoil converſation. But, do you ſay, Sir, there is no ſalvation to be had out of the pale of the catholick church.

Prieſt. 'Tis not my private opinion, all the great doctors of our church maintain it.

Duke. And by this catholick church, you mean the church of Rome, don't you ?

Prieſt. I do.

Duke. Why then, father, I am afraid you'll find it a hard matter to bring me to have a good opinion of her. *(Enter boy with the bottle and glaſſes.)* Set them down before us, and get you gone. Come, father, here's to his majeſty's good health.

Prieſt. I humbly thank your grace, but you have fill'd me too unmercifully, I can never----

Duke. Never take off ſuch a trifle ? you are no prieſt then. Come, I'll engage it never indiſpoſes you. What wou'd the king ſay to you, ſhould he know you refus'd his health ?

Prieſt. Well then I ſubmit : his majeſty's health, *(Drinks off his glaſs.)* And your grace's commands muſt never be diſputed.

Duke. But all this while, father, you take no *(playing with the cork)* notice of my fine gelding here. Do but obſerve his exquiſite ſhape : what a fine turn'd neck is there ? his eyes, how lively and

2   full ?

full? his pace, how majeſtick and noble? I'll lay
a hundred guineas, there's nothing in Newmarket
can compare with him.

Prieſt. An't pleaſe your grace, I ſee no horſe.

Duke. Why, don't you ſee me play with his
mane, ſtroke him under the belly, clap his but-
tocks, and manage him as I pleaſe?

Prieſt. Either your grace is merrily diſpoſed,
or elſe your illneſs has had a very unlucky effect
upon your grace's imagination. Upon my ſince-
rity I ſee nothing but a cork in your hands.

Duke. How! my horſe dwindled into a fooliſh
piece of cork? Come, father, this is very unkindly done of you, to turn the fineſt gelding in
Europe, whoſe ſire was a true Arab, and had a
better genealogy to ſhow than the beſt gentleman
in Wales or Scotland can pretend to: nay, whoſe
illuſtrious anceſtors have had the honour to carry
ſeveral Sultans of Babylon, Caliphs of Egypt,
Grand Signiors of Conſtantinople, and Xeriffs of
Morocco upon their backs; to turn, I ſay, a
creature ſo well deſcended into an idle cork.------
It ſurprizes me, it puts me into confuſion, I can't
tell what to ſay or do; therefore at my requeſt
once more obſerve him more carefully, and tell
me your opinion.

Prieſt. Not to flatter then this melancholy hu-
mour in your grace, which may but ſerve to confirm and rivet it the more in you, I muſt roundly
and fairly tell your grace, that 'tis a cork, and
nothing but a cork.

Duke. 'Tis hard, that a perſon of my quality's
word won't be taken in ſuch a matter, where I
have

have not the leaft profpeƈt of getting a farthing by impofing upon you; But, father, how do you make good your affertion ? I fay ftill 'tis a horfe, you tell me 'tis a cork ; how fhall this difference be made up between us ?

Prieſt. Very eafily; for inftance, I firft exa‑amine it *(taking the cork from the Duke)* by my fmell, and that tells me 'tis cork. I next confult my fight, and that affirms the fame: then I judge it by my tafte, and ftill 'tis cork. In fhort, my touch affures me 'tis cork, and my ears, that have heard the defcription of this bark a hundred times, concur in the fame ftory. 'Tis impoffible, that all my fenfes fhould be banter'd and cheated in an affair of this nature, and they are the proper judges to appeal to upon fuch occafions.

Duke. Nay, fince you are fo pofitive, father, I won't conteft the matter with you, but e'en let it be a cork. The fumes arifing from my illnefs, (which I thank you for not flattering) I perceive, had fomewhat difordered me: but now they are blown over, and I fee as plain as a pike ftaff that 'tis nothing but a cork.----So now, father, if you pleafe, to the bufinefs in hand.

Prieſt. I prefume your grace believes the Tri‑nity.

Duke. Hark you, father, before you proceed a ftep farther; thou'rt plaguily miftaken, if thou think'ft to make the Trinity a ftepping ftone to tranfubftantiation. I thought you came to recon‑cile me to thofe points about which the two churches differ; and not to fpend your breath, to no purpofe, upon a fubjeƈt wherein we are agreed.

Prieſt.

Prieſt. Be it ſo then, and ſince your grace has mention'd tranſubſtantiation, we'll enter into the merits of that controverſy. I need not remind your grace, that no article of our holy religion is ſo expreſsly laid down in ſcripture as that: for what can be plainer than, *Hoc eſt corpus meum ?*

Duke. But under favour, father, 'tis not ſo plain as you imagine. 'Tis certain the primitive chriſtians believed nothing of the matter, nor ever dreamt of a corporal preſence: for what tragical work would Lucian, Porphyry, Celſus, and the other learned adverſaries of chriſtianity, have made with the chriſtian apologiſts, who uſed to charge the pagans with the barbarity of their human ſacrifices, expoſe the *foible* of their deities, and droll upon old Saturn, for devouring his own children, had tranſubſtantiation been the avowed belief of thoſe primitive times? how wou'd they have inſulted the chriſtians, and turn'd off the edge of this recrimination from themſelves? could they have taxed the chriſtians with that moſt monſtrous, moſt abſurd, and moſt barbarous principle of eating the very God that made and redeem'd them?

Prieſt. How ver, this article, as abſurd and monſtrous as your grace repreſents it, has the countenance of fathers and œcumenical councils, and has been aſſerted by all the celebrated doctors of the Greek and Latin church; not to mention a conſtant ſeries of miracles, that have ſupported it ever ſince the inſtitution of our religion.

Duke. As for your fathers and councils, I value them not a farthing. They were men as well as we,

we, and confequently as liable to miftakes. Befides, I muft tell you plainly, 'tis not fair to mention them out of a library, where you may immediately be fatisfied whether the quotation is
honeft, or to any other but fuch who have carefully read them over in the originals; whereas,
'tis common with you priefts, to make a great
pother about them to tradefmen, and fea-men.
'Tis plain, the fathers, and councils were never
intended to be the regulators of our faith; for
three parts in four of mankind have neither capacity nor leifure to read them; and, of thofe few
that do, fewer underftand them, and even thofe
that pretend to underftand them are at endlefs
wars, whether they are genuine or no, and make
no fcruple to reject them when they don't ferve
their turn.

Prieft. To let your grace fee I am a fair adver-
fary, I will at prefent lay afide both fathers and
councils, and appeal even to your own tranflation
of the bible, where, at the inftitution of this my-
fterious facrament, our Saviour exprefsly tells his
difciples, *This is my body.*

Duke. So he tells them in the fame book, *I am
the door, and I am the vine*; and yet I never heard
that any fet of men, or any particular man, was
ever fo frantick as to maintain, that he was either
a door, or a vine, tho' they have as plain a text to
countenance it as you have for tranfubftantiation.
All thefe are figurative expreffions, fuch as daily
occur in common converfation, and none but fools
out of ignorance, or knaves out of intereft, inter-
pret them in the literal fenfe.-----But to difmifs

this

this digreffion, prithee tell me, honeſt father, whether, at the celebration of the laſt ſupper, our Saviour gave himſelf to be verily and really eaten by his diſciples?

Prieſt. No doubt on't; for what ſays St. Auſtin upon this occaſion? *Chriſtus portavit ſeipſum manibus ſuis.*

Duke. If that father was ſuch a coxcomb as to expreſs himſelf ſo fooliſhly, what's that to me?--- Well then, if our Saviour was really eaten by his diſciples at that ſupper, it follows of courſe, that he was really dead, and that he ſuffered death, and was made an oblation for the ſins of mankind, before he offered himſelf a victim to the juſtice of his father upon the croſs, which I ſuppoſe you will hardly maintain.

Prieſt. May it pleaſe your grace, theſe are myſteries, imparted to us by divine revelation, which we are with the utmoſt ſubmiſſion to believe, tho' they ſhock our reaſon and ſenſes never ſo much.

Duke. I ſee, father, I muſt refreſh your memory with this piece of cork, which I poſitively affirm once more to be a horſe: juſt now you would be governed by the ſenſes, in thoſe matters that properly belong to their tribunal, but now you diſown the juriſdiction of the court, which is not honeſtly done.

Prieſt. But in matters of faith.-----

Duke. And what of all that? No man ſhall ever perſuade me to believe againſt the plain conviction of my ſenſes-----Here's a conſecrated wafer; you tell me 'tis God Almighty: I ſay 'tis a piece of bread, and nothing elſe. If I examine it by my

taſte,

tafte, 'tis bread, if by my fmell, fight and touch, 'tis bread ftill. Now why, for the fake of a dubious phrafe, which is agreeable to fenfe and reafon when underftood metaphorically, but involves a million of contradictions and abfurdities when literally, fhould I fet up a moft monftrous and impious doctrine, in downright oppofition to common fenfe and reafon, to the end of our Saviour's fuffering upon the crofs, which was to be performed but once, and not daily, as you affert in ten thoufand different places, and laftly, to the majefty of the divine effence.

Prieft. My Lord Duke, you muft humble your reafon to reconcile yourfelf to this holy myftery, which even the angels themfelves don't comprehend.

Duke. Our Saviour, when he firft inftituted his religion, wrought feveral miracles before the people, by which he appealed to their fenfes, fo 'tis plain, that he thought 'em the proper judges of miracles. When you have a *Mahometan* or *Pagan* to convert, you tell him of thefe fame miracles, and that they could proceed from nothing but a divine power, and fo you get him into your church; but as foon as you have got him there, you preach up quite contrary doctrine; and tell him he muft renounce his reafon and fenfes, under pain of damnation. Thus you fubtilly appeal to his fenfes, to wheedle him into St. Peter's net; but when you have him fafe there, he muft truft to them no longer: nay, he muft lay them afide as enemies to the catholick truth.

Prieft. As abfurd as your Grace looks upon this

z   doctrine

doctrine to be, 'tis believed by the majority of the christian world.

Duke. That's worfe and worfe ftill; in all ages and nations of the world, error ever drew more profelytes after it than the truth-------But not to combat fo inhuman as well as nonfenfical a tenet any longer, I'll tell you a fhort ftory. When I was fent ambaffador from the late king to Paris, in the year 1670, I took over with me a young blackamore boy, who could juft make a fhift to be underftood in Englifh; and this boy, one holyday morning, went along with fome of my gentlemen to fee the curiofities of fo remarkable a city, and all of them at laft went into Notre-dame church, as the prieft was celebrating mafs, at the high mafs. The lad was perfectly furprized at their rich habits, and fine mufick; and when the prieft came to the elevation, he afked one of my gentlemen, what that white thing was which the man in the party-coloured coat held up in his fingers? Why, (replies he) thefe people believe it to be God Almighty. Not long after, at a fidealtar, he faw a prieft giving the wafer to a parcel of people upon their knees, and putting it into their mouths. What, (cries he to the gentleman) do they eat their God after they have fo folemnly worfhipped him? Yes, anfwers he, this is their belief. The boy was fo ftrangely confounded at what he had obferved, that he fpoke not a fyllable when he came home; but was moping and mufing by himfelf. I could not but take notice of this alteration in him at dinner. So Tom, fays I to him, what's the matter with thee? if thou'rt ill,

go

go down to the houſe-keeper : No, cries he, I am
not ſick; but I have ſeen a very odd ſight this
morning, which I can't help thinking on. I ſaw
a man in fine cloaths ſhow the people God, and
they fell upon their knees, and beat their breaſts;
and afterwards I ſaw this man put God into their
mouths, and they ſwallowed him. Well, ſays I,
and where's the harm of that, Tom? I don't
know, ſays the boy, why they ſhould eat God,
ſince he does us no harm; but, if they have the
ſame power over the Devil, I wiſh we had a hundred or two of theſe fine men in our country, to
eat the Devil for us; for we cannot reſt for him
a-nights, he pinches us in the arms, ſours our
palm-wine, ſpoils our victuals, and is ſo plaugy
miſchievous, he and his young cubs, that we
ſhould be glad to get rid of him at any rate.
And this reflection a poor ignorant lad juſt come
from Guinea made of himſelf.

Prieſt. I am ſorry to ſee your grace in a diſpoſi-
tion ſo unfit to receive thoſe ſublime truths; but,
pray, let me aſk you one ſober queſtion, is it not
ſafer, as well as more diſcreet, to fly into the
arms of a church that is infallible, than be guided
by a wandering meteor, by an *ignis fatuus ?* for
I never heard the gentlemen of your communion
pretend to be exempt from error.

Duke. That ſhows their modeſty, and I promiſe
you, father, to reply to you more particularly to
this point, when your doctors have agreed where
to lodge their infallibility. In the mean time, 'tis
not worth your while to talk of it; for I ſhall lead
you ſuch a wild-gooſe chaçe from general councils

to the conclave, and from thence to the cathedra, and fo back again, in an everlafting circle, that you'll foon be weary of the labyrinth.

Prieſt. Well, then, your grace cannot but own, that we are the only church that are poffeffed of the facred treaſure of miracles; and thefe are fuch evident deſtonſtrations of----

Duke. Well, father, fince we have fallen again, I don't know how, upon the chapter of miracles, I will take care to entertain you with one that happened but laſt winter in Northumberland, and comes confirmed from fo many hands, both catholick and proteſtant, that he muſt be a very rank infidel indeed, who dares difpute the credibility of it. But, as I have one of the moſt treacherous memories in the world, I won't pretend to relate it to you myfelf, but one of my fervants fhall do it---Here ; *(to one of his gentlemen coming into the room)* go bid long John come to me immediately.

Prieſt. Your grace may fave yourfelf that trouble, if you pleafe, for I am as well fatisfied as if I had heard it.

Duke. Nay, you're no prieſt for my money if you refufe to hear a miracle, and, what is more, a catholick miracle. *(long John enters)* Come, John, you muſt oblige this worthy gentleman here, who is come upon no lefs errand than the falvation of your maſter's foul, with the relation of that famous miracle that happened laſt winter in Northumberland.

John. Your grace had always a right to command me. Why, then, Sir, you are to underſtand, that within two miles of my Lord Widdrington's drington's houfe, in the above-mentioned county, there is a fmall village (I am forry I have forgot its name, but I hope I fhall recover it anon) which wholly belongs to his lordfhip; by the fame token moft of the inhabitants, in complaifance, I fuppofe, to their landlord, are Roman Catholicks.

Duke. Very well, proceed.

John. An ancient woman of this village was accidentally fitting at her door, about three in the afternoon, when my lord's prieft happened to brufh by her. She immediately ran after him, and told him, dear father, you muft never think of going to his lordfhip to-night, the ways are flippery, and full of floughs, the days are fhort, and you'll certainly be benighted before you can have got half the way thither; I tremble to think what would become of you, fhould you lofe the road, or fall into a ditch; therefore let me perfuade you to accept of a forry fupper and lodging at my houfe; I am fure my Lord will not be offended with you, and to-morrow you'll have the whole day before you.

Duke. And what reply made the prieft to all this?

John. After a little humming and hawing upon the matter, he confidered 'twould be his wifeft way to take up his quarters that night at the old woman's; fo he followed her to her houfe, fhe led him into a pretty fnug warm parlour, made him a fire nofe-high, then going into the yard, flew a barn-door fowl with her own hands, claped it on the fpit, and, when 'twas ready, neatly difhed up

with

with egg-fauce; and who fo chearful as fhe and
the prieft over their fupper ?

Duke. 'Twas well done.

John. Refolving to give fo worthy a gueft the
beft entertainment her houfe afforded, after fupper fhe prefented him with a difh of nuts of her
own gathering, and then thwacked his Guts with
apples and ale, and was very liberal of her nut-
meg and fugar. Thus they paffed away the hours
merrily: At laft bed-time approached. Our good
old landlady fhewed the father the chamber he
was to lie in, wifhed him a happy night, and de-
parted; but being a curious woman, as moft of
the fex are poffeffed with the fpirit of curiofity, fhe
peeped through the key-hole, to fee how the
prieft managed matters by himfelf.

Prieft. Honeft friend, you may drop your miracle here, if you pleafe, I'll hear no more
on't---

Duke. Father, your zeal has got the heels of
your difcretion. Upon my word, here's no trap
laid for a bawdy jeft; nothing, in fhort, but
what her majefty and maids of honour may hear.

John. To her infinite furprize and admiration,
fhe faw him jump, ftark naked as ever he was
born, not into the fheets, tho' they fmelt moft
delicioufly of lavendar and rofes, but into the
blankets. Down ftairs fhe hurries, full of grief
and confufion, which would not let her wink all
night; " And lord, cries fhe, what a wicked
" age is this we live in ? how cold and uncha-
" ritable, when a perfon of fuch merit and learn-
" ing, who has refided, too, fo long in the fa-
                                        " mily,

" mily, has not a fhirt to put on his back? I
" could never have thought my lord fo niggard-
" ly." Thefe afflicting thoughts, wholly occafioned by her zeal for religion and the profeffors
of it, made that impreffion upon her, that fhe did
not enjoy a minute's repofe that night. Early fhe
gets up next morning, and meafured out fix ells
of the fineft flaxen linen fhe had, which was of
her own fpinning. Prefently down comes the father. into the parlour; fhe inquires of him how
he paft the night, and was ravifhed with joy to
hear he had flept fo well. After this, comes in a
thundering toaft, with a full tankard of humming
ftale beer. The prieft and fhe foon ended it between them; and now fhe had courage enough to
tell him what fhe had obferved the night before.
Father, fays fhe, I beg your pardon for being
fo impudent as to peep through the key-hole laft
night; and truly I was griev'd to the heart, to fee
that a gentleman of your education and great
parts fhould be without a fhirt: come, never blufh
for the matter, I knew 'tis fo; but here are fix ells
of my beft linen, which will make you two very
good fhirts, and I humbly defire you to accept
of them.

Duke. Why, father, here's the quinteffence of
true chriftianity for you.

John. Well, daughter, replies he, I accept of
your prefent in good part, (for priefts and lawyers
are feldom guilty of refunding) not that I fhall
have any occafion of making ufe of it myfelf; for
you muft underftand, I belong to an order which
obliges us to wear woollen next our fkin, but it

may

may ferve to make towels for the altar, and the like, and therefore I will take it with me: then ordering the good woman to kneel, he gave her his benediction, and prayed, that, whatever she began to do after he was gone, she might continue a-doing till fun-fetting.

Duke. And what happened upon that?

John. Our landlady, little imagining that a miracle was entailed upon the father's blessing, very innocently fell to measure the small remainder of linnen she had left, when to her great astonishment, and that of her family, she continued in this posture till the fun was fet, and got fuch a prodigious quantity of linen by this means, that next week she was able to buy out her leafe, and is now the topping dame of the parish.

Duke. What think you now, father, of long John's story.

John. This miracle in a moment run thro' the four northern counties; every village and hamlet rung of it; nay, it croffed the Tweed, and filled the ears of the unbelieving Scots. The priest, wherever he came, was worshipped and respected like a little divinity, and the woman was magnified by all as a true pattern of primitive zeal, piety and charity, since heaven had been at the pains to reward her in so extraordinary a manner.

Priest. Honest friend, let me desire you to be as concise as you can, for, in plain truth, I am weary of your story already.

John. At the lower end of this village (where the above mentioned miraculous fcene happened) lived another old woman, a catholic likewise by
'perfuafion,

perfuafion, who, hoping to gain as much by
her godlinefs as her neighbour had done before
her, looked out as fharply for the father, as a
Yorkfhire Attorney does for a purfe-proud litigi-
ous client. At laft to her mighty fatisfaction fhe
fees him go by her door; immediately fhe trots
after him, tells him of the depth of the ways,
and the great danger he run of being loft, defires
him to confult his own fafety, and not expofe
himfelf to thofe cafualties which he might fo
reafonably expect from the badnefs of the ways,
and the darknefs of the nights. With thefe plau-
fible infinuations fhe wheedles the prieft into her
houfe, and to fecure him entirely to her intereft,
treats him with a fhoulder of mutton and a couple
of capons for fupper.

Duke. She took the right courfe to gain her
point, I muft needs own? for ever while you live,
father, tickle a prieft and a woman by the belly,
if you intend to make them yours.

John. When the table-cloth was taken away,
our cunning hypocrite, who was refolved to outdo her neighbour's entertainment in her provifions;
accordingly, brings in a double bottle of methe-
glin, fills a bumper, and begins profperity to the
catholic religion. She tells the father, that a
judicious perfon lately told her, that a cardinal
was coming from Rome, who was to make his
public appearance in Cheapfide, in cloth of
beaten filver and gold, marry was he, and that he
was to convert the whole nation, and then, father, (fays fhe) we fhall fee happy times. The
honeft prieft was fo taken up with his pot and pipe,

that

that he neither oppofed, nor feemed to approve her difcourfe. In this manner they drank and prattled till the liquor found a way into their pericraniums; they could hardly fee one another. The prieft, unable to hold up his head any longer, defired to be conducted to the room where he was to lie that night; the old woman, with much ado, gets him up ftairs, leads him to his bed, wifhes him a thoufand good-nights, and fo leaves him with a trufty jug of ale by his bed-fide, that if he waked in the night, he might have fomething to refrefh his confcience and thirft at once.

Duke. Well faid, John.

John. By that time the prieft had rigged himfelf and was come down into the parlour, cur antient matron had toffed up a nice breakfaft, out of the remainder of the capons, which, being highly feafoned, proved a very effectual fhoeing-horn for the other bumper. And now, with tears in her eyes, fhe began the fame ftory as her neighbour had done, lamenting the horrid ingratitude of the times, that fo learned and devout a man as he fhould want a fhirt; to prevent which for the future, as far as it lay within her fmall capacity, fhe made bold to make him a fmall prefent of a dozen ells of her beft linen cloth.

Prieft. You'll never have done, I'm afraid.

John. The prieft, who was not conjurer enough to dive into the bottom of her heart, to know whether fhe was guided by any mercenary by-ends, or whether her intentions were real, heartily thanked her for the noble prefent fhe had made
him,

him, and folding it up under his great coat, bid
her kneel down, and laying his facerdotal fift upon
her head, he gave her his bleffing; and prayed,
that whatever this good woman began to do after he was gone, fhe might continue a-doing till
fun-fetting.

Duke. And what fell out upon this?

John. The father was no fooner got over the
threfhold, but our matron, who had laid all her
tackle in readinefs, was going to meafure the remainder of her linen; but then confidering, upon
fecond thoughts, what a large morning-draught
fhe had taken with the prieft, and being a wife
prudent woman into the bargain, fhe thought it
would be convenient to make a little water before fhe fell to her work. She did fo, and continued in mingent circumftances from the morning till night, evacuating fo plentiful a ftream,
that fhe in a manner occafioned a fecond deluge.
In fhort, all the low-lands in Northumberland fuffered by it; twenty-four mills, upon ftrict examination, were found to be overwhelmed by this fudden inundation, befides cottages and hay-ricks
numberlefs. This old woman, confcious of her
own deceit and hypocrify, has not dared to fhow
her head among her neighbours fince this fatal
accident. All true catholics rejoice at the juft
difpenfation of heaven's favours, and fo my ftory
concludes.

Duke. Come, John, there's fomething to make
you amends for the pains you have taken. (John
bows, and quits the room.) Well, father, what's
your opinion now of this miracle.

Prieft.

Prieſt. Out of refpect to your grace, I was content to fit out the whole ſtory; though I gueſſed at firſt whereabouts it. would end. But fince your grace is pleaſed to demand my opinion, all I can ſay in the matter is, that. it was contrived on purpoſe to make us poor ſuffering catholicks ridiculous to the people.

Duke. Alas! poor ſufferers, in troth I pity you. However, father, I dare lay a. ſmall wager with you, that where your church has ſuffered once, ſhe has made the reformed ſuffer a hundred times. I need not deſcend to particulars, every country in Europe being able to bear teſtimony to this truth.

Prieſt. I find, then, I can expect to make no proſelyte of your grace.

Duke. Be aſſured, that neither you, nor any of your cloth will ever gain that point upon me---- I tell thee, father, frankly and freely, that were there no idolatry, nor ſuperſtition, nor cheating practiſed by thy church, as I am ſure there is, I would have nothing to do with her, while ſhe damns all that are not within her own pale, which is almoſt three parts in four of the globe. A church without charity, the diſtinguiſhing character of our religion, for all ſhe glitters with jewels and gold, is no chucrh for me, I promiſe you.

Prieſt. Though I have been unſucceſsful in my well-meant endeavours, yet I ſhall always continue to pray for your grace's converſion.

Duke. As for that, do as you pleaſe, it ſignifies nothing; but fail not to commend me to their majeſties, and tell them, that though I cannot
bring

bring myfelf to be of their perfuafion, yet they have not a more dutiful fubject in their three dominions than I am.

After a few compliments, his grace and the prieft parted.

The End of the Conference.

LETTERS.

L E T T E R S.

A SHORT DISCOURSE UPON THE REA-SONABLENESS OF MENS HAVING A RE-LIGION OR WORSHIP OF GOD.

To the R E A D E R.

WHEN I began to write upon this fubject, it was out of curiofity ; I had a mind to try what I could fay in reafon againft the bold affertions of thofe men, who think it a witty thing to defame religion : and I have feen fo few writings of late which are not very tedious, that I was defirous at leaft to avoid that fault in this, by making it as fhort as I could.

The reafon why I have fuffered it to be printed is, indeed, becaufe I could not help it ; copies having been taken of it, and fent to the prefs, by the negligence of fome to whom I lent it to read. I was as much afhamed to forbid the printing of it, as I fhould have been to have ordered it, or as I fhould be now it is printed to difown what I have written ; and therefore I have here fet my name to it.

By the nature of this difcourfe, I was forced to conclude with an opinion which I have been long

convinced,

convinced, That nothing can be more anti-chriftian, nor more contrary to fenfe and reafon, than to trouble and moleft our fellow chriftians, becaufe they cannot be exactly of our minds in all the things relating to the worfhip of God.

And who will but examine what multitudes of men there are now among us of different perfua-fions in religion, and how inconfiderable any one part of them is, compared to the reft, muft, I am confident, be convinced that the practice of it at this time would be of no advantage to the public.

If a ferious confideration of the prefent ftate of this kingdom can fink deep enough into mens hearts to make them endeavour how to promote a true liberty of confcience, I fhall yet hope to enjoy happy days in England; but otherwife, without pretending to be a prophet, I can eafily forefee that the contrary muft of neceffity termi-nate in this, a general difcontent, the difpeop-ling of our poor country, and the expofing it to the conqueft of a foreign nation.

BUCKINGHAM.

LETTER

L E T T E R I.

ADDRESSED TO NEVIL PAINE, ESQ.

THERE is nothing that gives men a greater dif-
fatisfaction, than to find themfelves difappointed
in their expectations, efpecially of thofe things, in
the having or not having of which they themfelves
are moft concerned. And therefore, all that go
about to give demonftrations in matters of religion, and fail in the attempt, do not only leave
men lefs devout than they were before, but alfo
with great pains and induftry lay in their minds
the grounds and foundation of atheifm; for the
generality of mankind, either out of lazinefs, or
diffidence of their being able to judge aright, in
points that are not very clear, are apt rather to
take things upon truft, than to give themfelves
the trouble to examine whether they be true or
no; but, when they find what a man undertakes
to give them for a demonftration is really none at
all, they do not only conclude that they are deceived by him, but begin to fufpect they have been
ill-ufed by thofe who firft impofed upon them a
notion, for which perhaps no demonftration can
be given, and from this fufpicion they run to another of a more dangerous confequence, that
what is not demonftrable, may alfo not be true.

I fhall therefore, in this fhort effay, make ufe
of another method; and content myfelf with en-
deavouring to fhew, what, in my opinion, is moft
propable; demonftration being as to matters of

VOL. II.   O   faith

faith abfolutely unnecefſary, becauſe if I can convince a man, that the notions I maintain are more
likely to be true, than falſe, it is not in his power not to believe 'em; no man believing any thing
becauſe he has a mind to believe it, but becauſe
his judgement is convinced, and he cannot chuſe
but believe it whether he will or no; and belief
is all that is required of us in the ſpeculative part
of religion : beſides, demonſtration being ſuch an
evidence of a thing as ſhews the contrary of it to be
impoſſible, it is, if you mark it, a pretty whimſi-
cal kind of expreſſion, to ſay, that a man does but
believe a thing to be ſo, which he is ſure cannot
poſſibly be otherways; 'tis juſt as ingenious as if
one ſhould profeſs, that he hopes he ſhall but begin to have a thing to-morrow, which he is already this day in poſſeſſion of, belief and faith being
as entirely ſwallowed up in demonſtration, as hope
is in fruition. My deſign, in this eſſay, is to induce men to a belief of religion by the ſtrength of
reaſon, and therefore I am forced to lay aſide all
arguments which have any dependence upon the
authority of ſcripture; and muſt faſhion my diſcourſe, as if I had to do with thoſe that have no
religion at all,

The firſt main queſtion, upon the clearing of
which I ſhall endeavour to ground the reaſonable-
neſs of mens having a religion, or worſhip of God,
is this: whether the world has ordered itſelf
to be as it now is, or was contrived to be ſo
by ſome other being of a more perfect, and more
deſigning nature ? for whether or no the world has
been created out of nothing, is not material to
our purpoſe ; becauſe if a ſupreme intelligent agent
                                                    has

has framed the world to be what it is, and has made us to be what we are, we ought as much to ſtand in awe of it, as if it had made both us and the world out of nothing: yet becauſe this latter queſtion ought not to be totally paſſed by, I ſhall take the liberty to offer ſome conceptions of mine upon it. The chief argument uſed againſt God Almighty's having created the world is, that no man can imagine how a thing ſhould be made out of nothing, and for that reaſon it is impoſſible he ſhould have made the world, becauſe there is no thing elſe out of which it could be made.

Firſt, Then, I cannot chuſe but obſerve, that to ſay, becauſe we are not able to imagine how a thing ſhould be, therefore the being of that thing muſt be impoſſible, is in itſelf a diſingenuous way of argumentation, eſpecially in thoſe who at the ſame time declare they believe this world to be eternal, and yet are as little able to comprehend how it ſhould be eternal, as how it ſhould be made out of nothing.

In the next place, I conceive, that nothing can be properly ſaid to endure any longer than it remains juſt the ſame; for in the inſtant any part of it is changed, that thing as it was before is no more in being. In the third place, that every part of this world we live in is changed every moment, and by conſequence that this whole world is ſo too; becauſe the whole is nothing elſe but what is compoſed of every part, and that therefore we cannot properly ſay, that this world has continued for many ages, but only that all things

in

in this world have been changed for several years together.

To evade which opinion, those, who maintain the eternity of the world, are forced to say, that the matter of it is not changed, but the accidents only, tho' this be a sort of argument, which they will not allow of in others; for when it is by Papists urged, in defence of transubstantiation in the sacrament, that the accidents of the wafer remain, though the substance of it be changed, they reject that as a ridiculous notion; and yet it is not one jot more absurd to say, that the accidents remain when the matter is changed, than that the matter remains when the accidents are changed: Nay, of the two, the asserters of this latter opinion are the least excusable; because they boldly attribute it to a natural cause, whereas the Papists have the modesty, at least, to own it for a miracle.

But that the weakness of this imagination of separating accidents from bodies may the plainer appear, let us examine a little what the meaning of the word accident is. Accident then does not signify a being distinct from body or matter; but it is only a word whereby we express the several ways we consider of what we find in a body or matter that is before us: for example, if we perceive a body to have length, then we consider that length as an accident of that body, and when we perceive a body to have a smell or taste, then we consider that smell and that taste as accidents of that body; but in none of these considerations do
we

we mean, that any thing can have length, fmell, or tafte, but what really is a body; and when any thing, that had a fmell or tafte, has left off to have a fmell or tafte, it is becaufe that part of it, which had a fmell or tafte, is no more in it; fo that upon a nice examination of the whole matter I am apt to believe this will appear to be the cafe; that there can be no changing of accidents, but where there is a real change of bodies.

But to proceed a little further, the queftion being, whether it be more probable, that this world, or that God Almighty has been from all eternity? I think I may venture to affirm, that of two propofitions the leaft probable is that which comes neareft to a contradiction; now nothing can come nearer to a contradiction, than that the fame being fhould be the fame for ever, and yet continually changed, or not abiding the fame one moment, and therefore I conclude it is lefs probable, that this changeable world fhould have been from all eternity, than that fome other being of more excellence, and greater perfection fhould be fo, whofe very nature is incapable of change.

That being, out of more excellence and greater perfection, I call *God*, and thofe who out of a foolifh averfion they have for the name of *God* will call it *nature*, do not in any kind differ from the notion of that being, but only change its name, and rather fhow they have a vain miftaken ambition of being thought Atheifts, than that they have any reafon ftrong enough to convince them to be fo.

O 3   The

The next queſtion I ſhall take into conſider-
ation is this, *Whether though there be a God, it is
probable that he ſhould take a more particular care of
mankind than he does of beaſts and other animals?*
To which I have this to offer, that though there
are ſeveral ſorts of animals which give us occaſion
to imagine they have ſome kind of reaſon in them,
though not to ſo great a perfection as men have,
yet ſince no other animal did ever any one thing
that could give us the leaſt cauſe to believe they
have a conception of another world, or of a
Deity; and that no man was ever yet born but
had a conception, or at leaſt a ſuſpicion of it more
or leſs.

I ſay, for this reaſon, it is as probable in my
opinion, that there is a ſomething near a-kin to
the nature of God in men than there is in any
other animal whatſoever, and for that reaſon that
God Almighty does take a more particular care
of us than he does of them.

If then God be eternal, and it is probable there
is ſomething in our nature which is a-kin to the
nature of God, it is alſo probable that that part
of us never dies.

It is alſo probable, that what by it we are
prompted moſt to value and eſteem as the higheſt
perfections, good qualities and virtues are parts of
the eſſence and nature of God. Now of all good
qualities or virtue it is juſtice which all men do
moſt highly eſteem and value in others, though
they have not all the good fortune to practiſe it
themſelves. For juſtice is that good quality or
virtue which cauſe all other good qualities or vir-

tues

tues to be efteemed, in us it is that virtue, without which all other virtues become as vices, that
is, they all come to be abhorred.

For he who wants juftice, and has wit, judgment, or valour, will for the having wit, judgment, or valour, be the more abhorred, becaufe
the more wit, judgment, or valour he has, if he
wants juftice, the more he will certainly become a
wicked man ; and he who wants juftice, and has
power, will for the having power be the more
abhorred, becaufe the more power he has, if he
wants juftice, the more he will certainly become a
wicked man ; and therefore, in my opinion, it is a
very unreafonable thing for men, out of a defign
of extolling God Almighty's power, to rob him
of juftice, the quality, without which even power
itfelf muft neceffarily be abandoned, and pray to
God Almighty than to fancy that he fhall punifh
us for doing that which he has from all eternity
predeftinated, that is, compelled us to do ? It is
an act that I can hardly believe there ever was a
man yet born cruel enough to be guilty of, even
in the depth of his revenge, and fhall we make
that attribute of the moft Perfect and moft High
God, which is beneath the effect of the meaneft
of paffions in the worft of men ? It is, in my opinion, more reafonable to believe that God Almighty, out of his love to mankind, has given
us an eternal foul, that an eternal being and free-
will are things in this nature infeparable one
from the other, and that therefore, according
to our actions, proceeding from our wills, God
Almighty, in juftice, will reward and punifh us

in

in another world for the good and evil deeds we perform in this. I do not fay that the beft of our actions here are good enough to make us deferve the utmoft joys of heaven; we muft owe that to God Almighty's grace and favour, as, indeed, we owe all things elfe, Neither will I take upon me to guefs at the feveral degrees of joys there are in heaven; our dull fenfe makes it impoffible for a man blind to talk well of colours. Nor will I pretend to judge how long or much God Almighty will punifh us hereafter, becaufe, for the fame rea-fon, that we think him to be a God of juftice, we muft alfo conclude him to be a God of mercy. This only, I do verily believe, that the more we love him the more he will love us, and the lefs we love him the worfe it will be for us.

Again, if this inftinct or conception we have of a Deity be the ground of our religion, it ought alfo to be the guide of our religion, that is, if the ftrongeft reafon we have to believe, that God Almighty does take a more particular care of us than he does of other animals, is, becaufe there is fomething in our natures nearer a-kin to the nature of God than any thing that is in other animals, I fay, in all reafon, that part of us which is neareft a-kin to the nature of God ought to be our guide and direction in chufing the beft way for our religious worfhip of God.

There is alfo this other confequence, which in my opinion does naturally depend upon what has been faid, That one of the greateft crimes a man can be guilty of, is to force us to act or fin againft that inftinct of religion which God Almighty has

placed

placed in our hearts ; for if that inftinct be fomewhat a-kin to the nature of God, the finning
againft it muft be fomewhat a-kin to the fin
againft the Holy Ghoft.

If then it be probable that there is a God, and
that this God will reward and punifh us hereafter, for all the good and ill things which we act
in this life, it does highly concern every man to
examine ferioufly which is the beft way of worfhip-
ping and ferving this God, that is, which is the
beft religion.

Now if it be probable, that the inftinct which
we have within us of a Deity, be a-kin to the nature of God, that religion is probably the beft
whofe doctrine does moft recommend to us thofe
things, which by that inftinct, we are prompted
to believe are virtues and good qualities ; and
that I think, without exceeding the bounds of
modefty, I may take upon me to affirm is the
chriftian religion ; and for the fame reafon it does
alfo follow, that the religion among chriftians,
which does moft recommend to us virtue and a
good life, is in all probability the beft religion.
And here I muft leave every man to take pains in
feeking out and chufing for himfelf, he only being anfwerable to God Almighty for his own foul.

I began this difcourfe, as if I had to do with
thofe who have no religion at all, and now ad-
dreffing myfelf to chriftians, I hope they will not
be offended at me, for ending it with the words
of our Saviour, *Afk and it fhall be given you, feek
and you fhall find, knock and it fhall be opened unto
you.*

I fhall

I shall beg leave further, only to propose a few questions, to all those in general who are pleased to call themselves christians.

First, Whether there be any thing more di-rectly opposite to the doctrine and practice of Jesus Christ, than to use any kind of force upon men, in matters of religion? and consequently, whether all those that practice it (let them be of what sect or church they please) ought not justly to be called Anti-christians?

Secondly, Whether there can be any thing more unmanly, more barbarous, or more ridiculous, than to go about to convince a man's judgment by any thing but by reason? It is so ridiculous, that boys at school are whipped for it, who in-stead of answering any argument with reason, are loggerheads enough to go to cuffs.

And *Thirdly*, Whether the practice of it has not always been ruinous and destructive to those countries where it has been used, either in monarchies or commonwealths? And whether the contrary practice has not always been successful to those countries where it has been used, either in mo-narchies or commonwealths?

I shall conclude, with giving them this friendly advice :---If they would be thought men of reason or of a good conscience, let them endeavour by their good council and good example, to persuade others to lead such lives as may save their souls, and not be perpetually quarrelling amongst themselves, and cutting one another's throats, about those things which they all agree are not abso-lutely necessary to salvation.

THE

THE DUKE OF BUCKINGHAM'S LETTER TO THE UNKNOWN AUTHOR OF A PAPER INTITULED, " A SHORT ANSWER " TO HIS GRACE THE DUKE OF BUCK- " INGHAM'S PAPER, CONCERNING RE- " LIGION, TOLERATION, AND LIBERTY " OF CONSCIENCE."

My namelefs, angry, harmlefs humble Servant,

I HAVE twice read over, with a great deal of patience, a paper of yours, which you call an anfwer to a difcourfe of mine, and to my confu-fion muft own, that I am not able to comprehend what part of my difcourfe it is you do anfwer, nor in all yours what it is you mean: But in this you are even with me, for I perceive you do as lit-tle underftand any part of what I have written, though I thought it had been done in fo plain a ftile, that a child of fix years old might very well have done it. Yet I do not take ill from you this art you have of mifunderftanding plain things, fince you have done the fame in his Majefty's promife to the church of England. The true meaning of which (without this mifunderftanding art of yours) would eafily have appeared to be, that he would not fuffer any body to injure the church of England, but he has not promifed that he would have the church of England perfecute every body elfe.

Having confeffed that I cannot underftand your writing, you ought not to be offended at me, if I

cannot

cannot remember it neither; and yet there is one paſſage in it which I ſhall never forget, becauſe it does in a moſt extraordinary manner delight me: It is this ſhrewd convincing argument of yours, which you ſay; *Had you been to treat with atheiſts, you would have urged to them, that it is impoſſible this world ſhould be eternal, becauſe then it muſt alſo be inviſible.* It is, I ſwear, a quaint kind of notion (which to do you juſtice) I do verily be-lieve it is entirely your own. Yet for all this, I cannot be abſolutely convinced that I am now the ſame George Duke of Buckingham which I was forty years ago; and to ſhew you I am in earneſt, I do here promiſe you, that if you will do for me a favour leſs difficult, which is to make me the ſame George Duke of Buckingham I was but twenty years ago, I will (as poor a man as I am) give you a thouſand guineas for your pains, and that is ſomewhat more I am afraid than you will ever get by your writing.

You have done me the honor to call yourſelf my humble ſervant, and therefore in gratitude I ſhall offer you an advice, which I am confident upon ſecond thoughts you will not find to be altogether unreaſonable: That hereafter, before you take upon you to write French, you will be pleaſed to learn the language, for the word *opinionature*, which you are ſo infinitely charmed with in your paper, has the misfortune to be no French word; the true French word which I ſuppoſed you would have uſed, is *opi-niatrete*, and yet I proteſt I do not ſee how (though you had written it right) it would have much more graced your diſcourſe than if it had been

expreſſed

expreffed in Englifh. Stick therefore to your
Englifh Metaphor, at which you are admirable,
and be always careful of not turning (according
to your own words) the wine of hope, into the
vinegar of defpair, and then you cannot fail of
being fufficiently applauded by every body, as
you are by

Your grateful friend,

BUCKINGHAM.

LETTER II.

TO MR. CLIFFORD, ON HIS HUMAN REASON.

YOUR little, but valuable book I have perufed
with a great deal of pleafure, tho' not without
fome concern; for while the truth it contained afforded me a manly fatisfaction, I was concerned
to reflect what enemies you would raife by fo honeft an attempt. The world is made up, for the
moft part, of fools or knaves, both irreconcile-
able foes to truth : The firft being flaves to a blind
credulity, which we may properly call bigotry:
The laft are too jealous of that power they have
ufurped over the folly and ignorance of the others,
which the eftablifhment of the empire of reafon
would deftroy. For truth, being made fo plain
and eafy to all men, would render the defigns and
arts of knaves of little ufe in thofe opinions, which
fet the world at odds and, by the feuds they maintain,

tain, enrich thofe who in a charitable peaceful world muft ftarve.

You muft expect, therefore, that the violent partifans of every fide will be your profeffed ene-mies; who, tho' they all pretend to be zealous of the truth, and to aim at its triumph over error; yet not one of them are for allowing any means of our arriving at it, but by giving into their princi-ples; for with each fide all truth is nothing bu their opinion : while that love and unity, which the divine love of the gofpel prefcribes, is the on-ly thing they all forget, and would perfuade the world out of, under the fpecious name of zeal for the orthodox : as if religion had its fundamen-tals in wrangling and obftinacy.

This has made each party fuch enemies to mo-deration and liberty of confcience, when it got to the helm; which, if once juftly and firmly efta-blifhed, would open the door to that peace which the gofpel was beftowed on us to introduce into the world. Lucretius, from his reflexion on the facrificing of Iphigenia, for a wind at Aulis, forms his celebrated Ephiphonema, *Tantum reli-gio potuit fuadere malorum.* But what would he have faid, if he had lived after the eftablifhment of the chriftian religion? Since the heats and ani-mofities betwixt the Arians and orthodox; the feveral opinions that ftarted up amongft them? When once the heathen folly was funk and re-moved, power foon debauched the principle, which Chrift gave us the character“iftic of his’dif-ciples, *the love of one another.* If he had feen how many millions of men loft their lives in the con-

I   tefts

tefts about the fupremacy of the popes; and the quarrels betwixt the emperors and the bifhops of Rome; or the one and twenty millions deftroyed by the Spaniards in the reduction of the Weft-Indies, who thought, in the fpreading their religion in thofe parts, the maxim of Mahomet preferable to that of Chrift, when they preferred the power of the fword to that of the gofpel, when they knocked fo many millions on the head, rather than be at the trouble of converting them. If he had known the noble methods of the inquifition of the Romanifts, and the penal laws of the reformed, by which in our nation alone, in a few years, threefcore thoufand families were ruined, he would have been no longer amazed at the facrificing one poor green-ficknefs girl.

But when the reformers had caft off the unfufferable bondage of Rome, and refcued the gofpel from the impofitions and impoftures of that church, one would have imagined they fhould have caft away that odious maxim of confining, and impofing on the confciences of thofe they had fet free; and never have dreamed of perfecuting them for making ufe of that liberty they had pretended to eftablifh, by requiring an implicit faith in them and their doctrines, when they would not allow it to thofe of the church they had forfaken for her errors and tyranny. For to me it is very unaccountable, that they fhould pretend to tell us, that we fhould now freely confult the word of God, and, at the fame time, deny us to underftand it for ourfelves; fince that is but to fool us with the name of liberty, without letting us

poffefs

poſſeſs the thing, and we might as well have continued under our old maſters, as be ſlaves to new lords. And this I believe has ſtopped the progreſs of the reformation. For when the firſt heat once was over, and conſidering men began to reflect, that the reformation offered nothiug but words, that it gave no entire freedom to conſciences and inquiries, they ſaw no ſatisfactory motive of quitting their old Mumſimus for a new Sumſimus, and could find no real advantage in wlthdrawing from father Peter, to father Martin and father John; ſince, though theſe diſclaimed the infallibility the other uſurped, yet they ſtill, without that guard, demanded our belief of their doctrines, though not leſs abſurd and ridiculous.

There is no way, indeed, left to make the reformation flouriſh, but its eſpouſing ſincerely a *true and perfect libery of conſcience*; that is, that it make the empire of reaſon ſacred, and not to be invaded by any party. But till this be effected, your book will be attacked on all hands by men that are ſo littlle friends to God and human kind, that they are for deſtroying the very diſtinction betwixt man and beaſt, that is, Reaſon; as if the God of Man and Reaſon could make it eſſential to religion, to make us ceaſe to be men.

For my part, I hope I am as good a chriſtian as any of theſe fiery gentlemen, and yet, from my peruſal of the bible, I can find no ground for ſo monſtrous a principle; nay, on the contrary, I can find no way of confuting the enemies of religion, the papiſts and atheiſts, but by reaſon, and the interpretation of ſcripture by that infallible guide. I çall it an infallible guide, becauſe

2   without

without its help we muſt continually wander in
the dark after the *ignis fatuus* of every opinion,
that can quote texts or authority for its ortho-
doxy. But, when we conſult that, all diſputes
ſoon ceaſe, and truth ſoon ſhines out as bright as
the noon-day ſun.

Moſt, if not all religious ſects, tell us, that a
true faith is neceſſary to ſalvation, and yet they
allow us no certain means of arriving at that true
faith. Now, it is contradictory to the very eſſence and being of a God, that he ſhould require
a true faith of us, and yet leave us no way to
arrive at it, nor any marks of the true faith,
which muſt inevitably be, unleſs you permit
us the free and uncontrouled uſe of our reaſon;
and that indeed will eaſily and ſoon, through the
New-Teſtament, lead us to the certain meaning
of Chriſt and his Apoſtles.

From what I have ſaid, you will find, that it is
my opinion that you have done a noble ſervice
to religion, in aſſerting the empire of reaſon, and
you have this comfort, that all thoſe, who have
any eſteem for the nobleſt of God's handy-works,
man, and any veneration for the wiſdom, vera-
city, and juſtice of God, will be your friends. And
then I need not deſcribe the quality, and nature
of your future antagoniſts. Nor have you in rea-
lity any cauſe to be alarmed at what they ſhall ſay.
You have too much ſenſe to value the cenſure of
fools, and too much honeſty to fear the rage of
knaves; elſe you could never have ſo near a place
in the love of, yours,

BUCKINGHAM.

LETTER III.

TO SIR HENRY THOMPSON.

A PERSUASIVE FROM HIS STANDING AGAINST
THE LORD TREASURER'S SON FOR BURGESS
OF YORK.

SIR,

HAVING promised to be your friend, I cannot but think myself obliged to be always very much concerned for you, and therefore I hope you will not take it ill, if I adventure to give you my advice, as often as I think it may be for your service: The noise of the dispute between you and my lord treasurer's son, about the being chosen burgess for the town of York, made me tell my lord treasurer the other day, that I thought he might make you the compliment of not letting his son stand in competition with you, considering how earnest you have been in the election of his lordship to the same burgess-ship before; upon which he shewed me a letter you wrote to him, wherein you owned yourself to be very sorry for having been forced to accept of it, by some aldermen of the town of York, and that you heartily wished to be disengaged from it by them. The only thing he seems to take ill of you is, that you would so hastily enter into this business, without giving him any notice of it; protesting withal, that, if you had, he would never have made the

least

leaſt mention of his ſon in the cafe. And as to
that point, I confeſs I did not well know what
to anſwer, ſince it was but a civility due to any
gentleman in England of the leaſt quality whatſoever. How far you are engaged in this I cannot
tell; but, let it be as far as it will, if I were in
your place, I ſhould not think the being choſen
at this time worth the diſobliging ſo conſiderable
a friend as my lord treaſurer is. In ſhort, if
this conteſt goes on, it will breed an irrecon-
cileable quarrel between you; and I cannot
for my life think that would be for your advantage, at leaſt I am ſure it would be very diſa-
greeable news to,
S I R,
You moſt affectionate friend,
and humble ſervant.

At the Cockpit,
Sept. 4. 1763.   BUCKINGHAM.

L E T T E R I.

TO THE LORD MAYOR AND ALDERMEN OF THE CITY OF YORK.

TO PERSUADE THEM TO CHUSE THE LORD TREA-
SURER'S SON FOR ONE OF THEIR BURGESSES.

My Lord, and Gentlemen,

UPON the anſwer of a letter I writ to Sir
Henry Thompſon, wherein I a adviſed him to
put a compliment upon my lord treaſurer in not
oppoſing his ſon's election to the burgeſs-ſhip
P 2   of

of the town of York, I am forced to addrefs myfelf to your lordfhip and your brethren, becaufe
he tells me, he would be very willing to give over
this conteft, if your lordfhip and the aldermen
would give him leave to do it. I know not for
what reafons you have refolved (as Sir Henry
Thompfon has informed me) to chufe none hereafter to ferve you in parliament, that are not of
your own corporation; but methinks, confidering
the zeal my lord treafurer has had for your fervice, and how much it may be now in his power
to fhew it, you ought not to begin at this time to
put that rule into practice, fince it would look,
as if you did it becaufe he had differved you in
that employment. I am fure no man can be more
paffionately zealous for the good of the town of
York than he is, of which I could give you fome
late unqueftionable demonftrations, but that it does
not become me to fpeak of it, becaufe I am concerned in it myfelf. This at leaft deferves, that you
fhould not put an affront upon him; which under favour it would be, if you fhould refufe to let his fon
ferve in his ftead, fince perhaps he is the firft man
of his quality who was ever denied that kindnefs,
upon a removal out of the houfe of commons,
into the houfe of peers. I come now to my
own part; I am fure I have never deferved your
unkindnefs, and if you have any confideration of
me, I defire you to fhew it, in not putting ne-
glect upon my lord treafurer, fince by it you would
lay an eternal difobligation upon,

My lord, and gentlemen,

Your moft affectionate,

And humble fervant,

BUCKINGHAM.

LETTER V.

TO SIR HENRY THOMPSON,

ABOUT BUYING A HOUSE AND GARDENS.

SIR,   Wothrop, Dec. 1.

I Have received your letter concerning the houfe and gardens near my Lord Fairfax's houfe in York, and though what is afked for them be perhaps more than they are worth, I fhall not ftick at the price, fo I be affured of the convenience of having the little back way behind the houfe ftopped up, without which I confefs I do not well know how I fhall be able to live there. I do therefore defire you to fend me word pofitively, whether it may be done or no; and how far the circumftance of its being called the king's highway makes it necef-fary for me to have fome grant of it of his Ma-jefty, that I may get it done when I am at Oxford, which will be in a few days, where I fhall not fail to releafe Captain Mountjoy, if he be not freed before I come. I am fo little able to make com-pliments to thofe I love, and I love you fo much, that I fhall ufe none to you, only in plain Englifh, like an honeft country gentleman, I fhall affure you that I am, with all my heart,

Your moft affectionate friend and fervant,

BUCKINGHAM,

P 3   LET.

LETTER VI.

TO THE SAME.

ABOUT AN OBLIGING ORDER OF THE LORD MAYOR
AND CITY OF YORK IN HIS FAVOUR, AND
OTHER THINGS.

SIR,   Jan. 2d, 1665,

I Cannot exprefs to you, how extremely I am
pleafed at the order I received from my Lord
Mayor and the city of York, concerning the lane
behind my houfe; and though the convenience I
fhall receive by it be very great, yet I affure you
the demonftration it gives me of their kindnefs
is that in it which I value, and efteem moft.
When your letter came to me, I, being upon my
remove to Oxford, thought it beft to defer the
fending you an anfwer till my arrival there, in
hopes that I might, at the fame time, fend you
fome good news of what the city of York has fo
often recommended to me, and which I fhall in-
duftrioufly labour for, whether I be concerned in
it or no: but meeting with the Duke of Monmouth and my Lord Arlington upon the way,
they perfuaded me to come with them to my Lord
Croft's houfe, a few miles diftant from this place;
fo that I am forced to defire you to make my
excufe to my Lord Mayor, for not writing to him
fooner: I have appointed Jackfon, my Bailiff at
Honfly, to wait upon you, and receive your direc-
tions for the drawing fuch a paper, as will be re-
quifite

quifite for finifhing that favour which the city of
York are refolved to do me. As for the little
houfe and gardens on the other fide of the lane, I
fhall not meddle with them at prefent, fince they
are held at fo high a rate ; but I defire you to conclude a bargain immediately for the other houfe
on the left-hand, as you come in, and for the clofe
that belongs to it, on the other fide of the land,
where I intend to have my ftables, and I fhall
immediately provide the money. I hope I need
not tell you that I love you, I fhould be very unworthy if I were not from the bottom of my
heart,

S I R,

Your moft trufty, affectionate fervant,

BUCKINGHAM.

L E T T E R VII.

TO THE SAME.

A LETTER OF RECOMMENDATION.

S I R,   London, March 8.

THE bearer came up to town about a bufinefs
he will acquaint you with ; if there be any probability, that the man's intelligence at York be true,
I fhall do what he defires ; but I would not be engaged upon a foolifh thing, and therefore I defire
you to examine the man for me. He is a prifoner

P 4

now

now at York, and his name is Laffels, of which this bearer will give you an account. I am,

Your moft affectionate friend and fervant,

BUCKINGHAM.

LETTER VIII.

TO THE RIGHT HONOURABLE THE EARL OF AR-
LINGTON, PRINCIPAL SECRETARY OF STATE
TO HIS MAJESTY.

[Written by his Grace when he was Ambaffador at the Court of France.]

MY LORD,   St. Germains, Auguft 15, 1670.

IF I had had the good fortune to bring my Lord Faulconbridge's fecretary with me, he would have entertained your lordfhip with a whole fheet of paper full of the particulars of my reception here; for, I have had more honours done me, than ever were given to any fubject. You will receive, in two or three days, a propofition from this court, concerning the making war upon Holland only, which you may enlarge as you pleafe. *Monfieur de Lionne* fhewed me the model of it laft night, and I fhall fee the particulars before they are fent.

In the mean time, having not your cypher, I fhall only tell you in general, that nothing but our being mealy-mouthed can hinder us from find-ing our accounts in this matter : for you may almoft

moſt aſk what you pleaſe. I have written more at large in cypher to my lord Aſhley, and when you have diſcourſed together, if you think my ſtay here will be of uſe to his Majeſty, let me know it; if not, I will come away. I am,

> My Lord,
>> Your Lordſhip's moſt humble
>>> And moſt faithful ſervant,
>>>> BUCKINGHAM,

L E T T E R IX,

TO THE SAME.

MY LORD,   St. Germains, Auguſt 17.

I Have nothing to add to what I writ laſt, but that I am every day convinced of the happy con-juncture we have at preſent in our hands, of any conditions from this court, that we can in reaſon demand. The King of France is ſo mightily taken with the diſcourſes I make to him of his greatneſs by land, that he talks to me twenty times a-day; all the courtiers here wonder at it, and I am very glad of it, and am very much,

> My Lord,
>> Your Lordſhip's moſt humble
>>> And moſt faithful ſervant,
>>>> BUCKINGHAM.

LET-

L E T T E R X.

TO THE LORD BERKLEY.

My Lord,

I Muſt needs beg your lordſhip's excuſe, for not waiting upon you next Sunday at dinner, for two reaſons; the firſt is, becauſe Mrs. -------- refuſes to hear me preach; which I take to be a kind of a ſlur upon ſo learned a divine as I am: the other, that Sir Robert G------ is to go into the country upon Monday, and has deſired me to ſtay within to-morrow, about ſigning ſome papers, which muſt be diſpatched, for the clearing ſo much of my eſtate, as (in ſpite of my own negligence, and the extraordinary perquiſites I have received from the court) is yet left me. I'm ſure your Lordſhip is too much my friend, not to give me leave to look after my temporal affairs, if you but con-ſider how little I am like to get by my ſpirituality, except Mrs. B------ be very much in the wrong: pray tell her, I am reſolved hereafter never to ſwear by any other but by * Jo. Aſh; and if that be a ſin, it's as odd a one as ever ſhe heard of. I am,   My Lord,

Your Lordſhip's moſt humble,

And moſt faithful ſervant,

BUCKINGHAM.

* A box-keeper of the play-houſe.

SPEECHES

SPEECHES

IN

PARLIAMENT.

The Duke's Speech in a Conference between the
Houfes of Lords and Commons, concerning a
Difpute between the Eaft-India Company and
Mr. Skinner, 1668.

Gentlemen of the Houfe of Commons,

I Am commanded by the Houfe of Peers to open
to you the matter of this conference ; which is a
tafk I could wifh their Lordfhips had laid upon
any body elfe, both for their own fakes and mine :
having obferved in the little experience I have
made in the world, that there can be nothing of
greater difficulty than to unite men in their opinions whofe intereft feems to difagree. This,
gentlemen, I fear is at prefent our cafe ; but yet
I hope, when we have a little better confidered of
it, we fhall find, that a greater intereft does oblige
us, at this time, rather to join in prefervation of
both our privileges, than to differ about the vio-
lation of either. We acknowledge it is our intereft
to defend the right of the commons ; for fhould
we fuffer them to be oppreft, it would not be long
before it might come to be our own cafe ; and I
humbly conceive it will alfo appear to be the intereft of the commons to uphold the privilege of
the lords, that fo we may be in a condition to ftand

by

by and fupport them. All that their lordfhips
defire of you on this occafion is, that you will
proceed with them as ufually friends do when they
are in difpute one with another ; that you will not
be impatient of hearing arguments urged againft
your opinions, but examine the weight of what is
faid, and then impartially confider, which of us
two are the likelieft to be in the wrong. If we
are in the wrong, we and our predeceffors have
been in the wrong thefe many hundred years; and
not only our predeceffors, but yours too: this
being the firft time that ever an appeal was made,
in point of judicature, from the Lords houfe to
the houfe of Commons. Nay, thofe very Commons that turned the Lords out of this houfe,
though they took from them many other of their
privileges, yet left them the conftant practice of
this till the very laft day of their fitting. And
this will be made appear by feveral precedents
thefe noble Lords will lay before you, much better
than I can pretend to do. Since this bufinefs has
been in agitation, their Lordfhips have been a
little more curicus than ordinary, to inform themfelves of the true nature of thefe matters now in
queftion before us; which I fhall endeavour to
explain to you as far as my fmall ability, and my
averfion to hard words, will give me leave. For
howfoever the law, to make it a myftery and a
trade, may be wrapt up in terms of art, yet it is
founded upon reafon, and is obvious to common
fenfe. The power of judicature does naturally
defcend, and not afcend; that is, no inferior
court can have any power which is not derived to
it

it from fome power above it. The king is, by the laws of this land, fupreme judge in all caufes ec- clefiaftical and civil. And fo there is no court; high or low, can act but in fubordination to him ; and though they do not all iffue out their writs in the king's name, yet they can iffue out none but by virtue of fome power they have received from him. Now every particular court has fuch a par- ticular power as the king has given it, and for that reafon has its bounds : but the higheft court in which the king can poffibly fit, that is, his fu- preme court of lords in parliament, has in it all judicial power, and confequently no bounds : I mean no bounds of jurifdiction ; for the higheft court is to govern according to the laws, as well as the loweft. I fuppofe none will make a queftion, but that every man and every caufe is to be tried accord- ing to Magna Charta, that is, by his peers, or ac- cording to the laws of the land : and he that is tried by the ecclefiaftical courts, the court of admiralty, or the high court of lords in parliament, is tried as much by the laws of the land, as he that is tried by the king's-bench or common-pleas.' When thefe inferior courts happen to wrangle among themfelves, which they muft often do, by reafon of their being bound up to particular caufes, and their having all equally and earneftly a defire to try all caufes themfelves, then the fupreme court is forced to hear their complaints, becaufe there is no other way of deciding them. And this, un- der favour, is an original caufe of courts, though not of men. Now thefe original caufes of courts muft alfo of neceffity induce men, for faving of charges,

charges, and for difpatch fake, to bring their
caufes originally before the fupreme court: but
then the court is not obliged to receive them, but
proceeds by rules of prudence, in either retain-
ing or difmiffing them, as they think fit. This is,
under favour, the fum of all that your precedents
can fhew us ; which is nothing but what we practife every day; that is, that very often, becaufe
we would not be molefted with hearing too many
particular caufes, we refer them back again to
other courts : and all the arguments you can poffibly draw from hence, will not in any kind leffen
our power, but only fhew an unwillingnefs we
have to trouble ourfelves often with matters of
this nature. Nor will this appear ftrange, if you
confider the conftitution of our houfe, it being
made up, partly of fuch, whofe employments will
not give them leifure to attend the hearing of private caufes; and entirely of thofe that can receive
no profit by it. And the truth is, the difpute at
prefent is not between the houfe of lords and the
houfe of commons, but between us and Weftminfter-hall : for, as we defire to have few or no
caufes brought before us, becaufe we get nothing
by them, fo they defire to have all caufes brought
before them, for a reafon a little of the contrary
nature. For this very reafon it is their bufinefs
to invent new ways of drawing caufes to their
courts, which ought not to be pleaded there. As
for example, this very caufe of Skinner, that is
now before us, (and I do not fpeak this by rote,
for I have the opinion of a reverend judge in the
cafe, who informed us of it the other day in the
houfe)

houfe) they have no way of bringing this caufe
into Weftminfter-hall, but by the following form,
the reafon and fenfe of which I leave you to judge
of; the form is this : That, inftead of fpeaking,
as we ordinary men do that have no art, that Mr.
Skinner loft a fhip in the Eaft-Indies, to bring this
into their courts, they muft fay, " Mr. Skinner
" loft a fhip in the Eaft-Indies, in the parifh of
" Iflington, in the county of Middlefex." Now
fome of us lords, that did not underftand the re-
finednefs of this ftile, began to examine what the
reafon of this fhould be; and fo we found, that
fince they ought not by right to try fuch caufes,
they are refolved to make bold not only with our
privileges, but the very fenfe and language of the
whole nation. This I thought fit to mention,
only to let you fee, that this whole caufe, as well
as many others, could not be tried properly in any
place but at our bar ; except Mr. Skinner fhould
take a fancy to try the right of jurifdiftion between Weftminfter-hall and the court of admiralty,
inftead of feeking relief for the injuries he had received in the place only where it was to be given
him. One thing I hear is much infifted upon,
which is, the trial without juries; to which I
could anfwer, That fuch trials are allowed of in
the chancery and other courts ; and that when
there is occafion for them, we make ufe of juries
too, both by directing them in the king's-bench,
and having them brought up to our bar. But I
fhall only crave leave to put you in mind, that if
you do not allow us, in fome cafes, to try men
without juries, you will then abfolutely take away

the ufe of impeachments, which I humbly conceive you will not think proper to have done at
this time.

THE DUKE'S SPEECH IN THE HOUSE OF COMMONS,

Upon occafion of fome Queftions propofed by them
to his Grace, together with his Reply thereunto,
in Relation to feveral Mifmanagements of State
Affairs, by Advice of fome of the Miniftry, Ja-
nuary the 14th, 1673-4.

[The Duke being called into the Houfe, after
having given his Refpects to the Speaker, and of
each Hand, and behind him, expreffes himfelf
in thefe Words :

MR. SPEAKER,

I GIVE the houfe my humble thanks for the
honour you have twice done me, efpecially ex-
prefling myfelf fo ill yefterday. I hope you will
confider the condition I am in, in danger of paff-
ing in the cenfure of the world for a vicious perfon,
and a betrayer of my country : I have ever had the
misfortune to bear the blame of other men's
faults. I know the revealing the king's councils,
and correfponding with the king's enemies, are
laid againft me ; but I hope for your pardon if I
fpeak truth for myfelf. I told you yefterday, if
the triple league had any advantage in it (I fpeak
it

it without vanity) I had as great a hand in it as any man. Then upon the inftance of the French ambaffador, I was fent into France upon the fad fubject of condoling the death of madam, where I urged, for the fervice of the king, that the French ought not to endeavour to make themfelves confiderable at fea, of whom we had reafon to be more jealous than of the Dutch; becaufe the French then would have power to conquer us. When I returned, I found all demonftrations that the French had no fuch thoughts, but that the king of England fhould be mafter at fea. I do not pretend to judge whether I or other men were in the right, I leave the judgment of that to this honourable houfe. At this time my lord Shaftfbury and myfelf advifed not to begin a war without the advice of the parliament and the affections of the people, (for I look upon the king at the head of his parliament, to be the greateft prince in the world;) this was my lord Shaftfbury's opinion and mine, but not my lord Arlington's. My next advice was, not to make ufe of French fhips; half their value in money would have been more ferviceable. I alleged they would be of no ufe to us, by reafon of their want of experience in our feas, and there would be great danger in their learning the ufe of them; which advice my lord Arlington oppofed, notwithftanding the king was fo defirous of avoiding a breach with France, that he fent me to Dunkirk, and my lord Arlington to Utrecht, where I ftill endeavoured to get money inftead of fhips. At my firft audience, the king of France was willing to comply; but, after fome returns and letters

from hence, he was altered; but I make no re-
flexions upon perfons, but barely ftate matters of
fact. Then it was my lord Shaftfbury's advice and
mine, fo to order the war, as that the French
fhould deliver us fome towns of their conquefts
into our hands: an ufeful precaution in former
times. My lord Arlington would have no towns
at all for one year. And here is the caufe of the
condition of our affairs. We fet out a fleet with
intention to land men in order to the taking of
towns. The French army go on conquering, and
get all, and we get nothing, nor agree for any.
Pray confider who it was that was fo often locked
up with the French Ambaffador. My fpirit moves
me to tell you, that, when we were to confider
what to do, we were to advife with the French
ambaffador. I will not trouble you with reports,
but pray look not upon me as a peer, but an honeft
Englifh gentleman, who has fuffered much for
my love to my country. I had a regiment given
me, which was Sir Edward Scot's; I gave him
1600 *l.* for it: there is no popifh officer in it, nor
Irifhman. I fhall fay nothing of my extraordinary
gains, I am fure I have loft as much eftate as fome
men have gotten; (and that is a big word;) I am
honeft, and when I appear otherways, I defire to
die. I am not the man that has gotten by all this;
yet after all this I am a grievance: I am the
cheapeft grievance this houfe ever had; and fo I
humbly afk the pardon of the houfe for the trouble
I have given.

The fpeaker then proceeded to afk the Duke the
following queftions, by order of the houfe.

Queftion

Queſtion I. propoſed to the Duke.

Whether any perſons declared to your grace any ill advices againſt the liberties and privileges of this houſe, or to alter the government, who they were, and what they adviſed?

Anſ. There is an old proverb, Mr. Speaker, *over boots over ſhoes.* This reflects upon one that is not now living, and ſo I deſire pardon for not ſaying any thing farther, fearing it may be thought a malicious invention of mine, the perſon being dead. I have ſaid nothing yet but what I can juſtify, but this I cannot.

Queſ. II. *Some words fell from your grace yeſterday, wherein you were pleaſed to ſay ſome had gotten* 3, 4, 500,000 *l. The houſe would know who they were, and by what means they had gotten ſuch ſums.*

Anſ. I am not well acquainted by what means they got ſo much, being not at all acquainted with the ways of getting money. What the duke of Ormond has got is upon record, being about 500,000 *l.* my lord Arlington has not got ſo much, he has got a great deal.

Queſ. III. *By whoſe advice was the army raiſed, and Monſieur Schomberg made General?*

Anſ. I cannot ſay by whoſe advice, but, upon my honour, not by mine. I was told by a man that is dead, that my lord Arlington ſent for him, and it will be eaſily proved.

Queſ. IV. *By whoſe advice was this army brought up to awe the debates and reſolutions of the houſe of commons?*

Anſ.

Anf. I muft make to this the fame anfwer as I did before; it was a difcourfe from a man dead of one now living. If I had deferved the honour, I think I might have had the command of that army before him; but Schomberg was told, my lord Arlington would have the government by an army.

Quef. V. *Who made the French league?*

Anf. My lord Arlington and myfelf were only employed to treat, and finding the danger we were in of being cheated, we preffed the ambaffadors to fign before they had power; and though it was an odd requeft, yet they did fign.

Quef. VI. *Who made the firft treaty with France, by which the triple alliance was broken?*

Anf. I made that treaty.

Quef. VII. *By whofe advice was the Exchequer fhut up, and the order of payment there broken.*

Anf. I was not the advifer; I am fure I loft 3000 l. by it.

Quef. VIII. *Who advifed the declaration in matter of religion?*

Anf. I do not difown that I advifed it; being always of opinion, that fomething was to be done of that nature in matters of confcience, but no farther than the king might do by law.

Quef. IX. *Who advifed the attacking the Smyrna fleet before the war was proclaimed?*

Anf. It was my lord Arlington's advice, I was utterly againft it, as careful of the honour of the nation, and incurred fome anger by it. My lord Arlington principally moved it, and I might fay more.

Quef,

Quef. X. *By whofe advice was the fecond treaty at Utrecht ?*

Anf. My lord Arlington and I were fent over, and I found in Holland the greateſt conſternation imaginable, like the burning of the rump in England, the people crying, God bleſs the king of England, and curſing the States; and had we then landed, we might have conquered the country. The prince of Orange would have had the fame ſhare in the peace with France that we had; but, though the king's nephew, I thought he muſt be kind to his own country; if we had made a peace then, we had been in a worſe condition than before; and laſtly, the prince of Orange hoped for a good peace with us upon that treaty; but I would never conſent that France muſt have all and we nothing. The confequence would be that Holland muſt intirely depend upon France, and I think it a wife article, that the French were not to make peace without us.

Quef. XI. *By what counfel was the war begun without the parliament, and thereupon the parliament prorogued?*

Anf. My lord Shaftſbury and I were for adviſing with the parliament, and averfe to the prorogation. I can ſay nothing, but I believe the parliament will never be againſt a war for the good of England.

Then the debate followed.

THE DUKE'S SPEECH IN THE HOUSE OF LORDS, 16th NOVEMBER 1765, FOR LIBERTY OF CONSCIENCE.

My Lords,

THERE is a thing called liberty, which (whatever fome men may think) is what the people of England are fondeft of, it is what they will never part with, and it is what his majefty, in his fpeech, has promifed us to take a particular care of. This, my Lords, in my opinion, can never be done without giving an indulgence to all Proteftant diffenters. It is certainly a very uneafy kind of life to any man, that has either chriftian charity, humanity, or good nature, to fee his fellow-fubjects daily abufed, divefted of their liberties and birth-rights, and miferably thrown out of their poffeffions and free-holds, only becaufe they cannot agree with others, in fome opinions and niceties of religion, which their confciences will not give them leave to confent to; and which even by the confeffion of thofe who would impofe them upon them, are no ways neceffary to falvation. But, my Lords, befides this, and all that may be faid upon it, in order to the improvement of our trade, and increafe of the wealth, ftrength, and greatnefs of this nation, (which, under favour, I fhall prefume to difcourfe of fome other time) there is, methinks, in this notion of perfecution a very grofs miftake, both as to the point of government, and the point of religion

ligion. There is fo, as to the point of government, becaufe it makes every man's fafety depend on the wrong place, not upon governors, or a man's living well towards the civil government eftablifhed by law, but upon his being tranfported with zeal for every opinion that is held by thofe who have power in the church then in fafhion; and it is, I conceive, a miftake in religion, becaufe it is pofitively againft the exprefs doctrine and example of Jefus Chrift. Nay, my Lords, as to our proteftant religion there is fomething in yet worfe: for we proteftants maintain, that none of thofe opinions which chriftians differ about are infallible; and therefore it is in us a fomewhat inexcufable conception, that men ought to be deprived of their inheritance, and all the certain conveniencies and advantages of life, becaufe they will not agree with us in our uncertain opinions of religion. My humble motion therefore to your lordfhips is, that you would give me leave to bring in a bill of indulgence to all diffenting proteftants. I know very well, that every peer of this realm has a right to bring into parliament any bill he conceives to be ufeful to this nation; but I thought it more refpectful to your lordfhips to afk your leave for it before. I cannot think the doing of it will be of any prejudice to the bill, becaufe I am confident the reafon, the prudence, and the charitablenefs of it will be able to juftify itfelf to his houfe and the whole world.

THE

THE DUKE'S SPEECH IN THE HOUSE OF LORDS, TO PROVE THE PARLIAMENT DISSOLVED.

My Lords,

I Have often troubled your Lordſhips with my diſcourſe in this houſe; but I confeſs I never did it with more trouble to myſelf than I do at this time; for I ſcarce know where I ſhould begin, or what I have to ſay to your Lordſhips: on the one ſide, I am afraid of being thought an unquiet and pragmatical man; for in this age, every man that cannot bear every thing is called unquiet; and he that does aſk queſtions, for which we ought to be concerned, is looked upon as pragmatical. On the other ſide, I am more afraid of being thought a diſhoneſt man; and of all men, I am moſt afraid of being thought ſo by myſelf; for every one is the beſt judge of the integrity of his own intentions; and tho' it does not always follow, that he is pragmatical whom others take to be ſo; yet this never fails to be true, that he is moſt certainly a knave, who takes himſelf to be ſo. No body is anſwerable for more underſtanding than God Almighty has given him; and therefore, tho' I ſhould be in the wrong, if I tell your Lordſhips truly and plainly what I am really convinced of, I ſhall behave myſelf like an honeſt man: for it is my duty, as long as I have the honour to ſit in this Houſe, to hide nothing from your lordſhips, which I think may concern his Majeſty's ſervice, your Lordſhips intereſt, intereft, or the good and quiet of the people of England.

The queftion, in my opinion, which now lies before your Lordfhips, is not what we are to do, but whether at this time we can do any thing as a Parliament, it being very clear to me, that the Parliament is diffolved: and if in this opinion I have the misfortune to be miftaken, I have another misfortune joined to it, for I defire to maintain the argument with all the lawyers in England, and leave it afterwards to your Lordfhips to decide, whether I am in the right or no. This, my Lords, I fpeak not out of arrogance, but in my own juftification; becaufe if I were not thoroughly convinced, that what I have now to urge is grounded upon the fundamental laws of England, and that the not preffing it at this time, might prove to be of a moft dangerous. confequence, both to his Majefty and the whole nation, I fhould have been loth to ftart a notion, which perhaps may not be very agreeable to fome people. And yet, my Lords, when I confider where I am, whom I now fpeak to, and what was fpoken in this place about the time of the laft prorogation, I can hardly believe what I have to fay will be diftafteful to your Lordfhips.

I remember very well, how your Lordfhips were then difpleafed with the Houfe of Commons, and I remember too as well, what reafons they gave you to be fo. It is not fo long fince, but that I fuppofe your Lordfhips may call to mind, that, after feveral odd paffages between us, your Lordfhips were fo incenfed, that a motion was
made

made here for an addrefs to his Majefty about the
diffolution of this Parliament; and though it failed
of being carried in the affirmative by two or three
voices, yet this in the debate was remarkable,
that it prevailed much with the major part of
your lordfhips that were here prefent, and was
only overpowered by the proxies of thofe Lords
who never heard the arguments. What change
there has been fince, either in their behaviour,
or in the ftate of our affairs, that fhould make
your Lordfhips change your opinion, I have not
yet heard. And therefore if I can make it appear
(as I prefume I fhall) that by law the parliament
is diffolved, I prefume your Lordfhips ought not
to be offended at me for it.

I have often wondered how it fhould come to
pafs, that this Houfe of Commons, in which there
are fo many honeft, and fo many worthy gentlemen, fhould yet be lefs refpectful to your Lordfhips, as certainly they have been, than any Houfe
of Commons that were ever chofen in England;
and yet if the matter be a little enquired into,
the reafon of it will plainly appear. For, my
Lords, the very nature of the Houfe of Commons is
changed: they do not think now that they are an
affembly that are to return to their own homes,
and become private men again (as by the laws of
the land, and the ancient conftitution of parliaments they ought to be) but they look upon themfelves as a ftanding fenate, and as a number of men
pick'd out to be legiflators for the reft of their lives.
And if that be the cafe, my Lords, they have reafon to believe themfelves our equals. But, my
Lords,

Lords, it is a dangerous thing to try new experiments in a government: men do not forefee the ill confequences that muft happen, when they go about to alter thofe effential parts of it upon which the whole frame depends, as now in our cafe, the cuftoms and conftitutions of parliament: for all governments are artificial things, and every part of them has a dependance one upon another. And it is with them as with clocks and watches, if you fhould put great wheels in place of little ones, and little ones in the place of great ones, all the movement would ftand ftill: fo that we cannot alter any one part of a government without prejudicing the motions of the whole.

If this, my Lords, were well confidered, people would be more cautious, how they went out of the old, honeft, Englifh way and method of proceeding. But it is not my bufinefs to find fault, and therefore if your Lordfhips will give me leave, I fhall go on to fhew you, why in my opinion we are at this time no parliament. The ground of this opinion of mine is taken from the ancient and unqueftionable ftatutes of this realm; and give me leave to tell your Lordfhips, by the way, that ftatutes are not like women, for they are not one jot the worfe for being old. The firft ftatute that I fhall take notice of, is that in the 4th year of Edward III. chap 14. thus fet down in the printed book : " Item, it is accorded, that a parliament " fhall be holden every year once, and more often, " if need be. Now tho' thefe words are as plain as a pike-ftaff, and no man living; that is not a fcholar, could poffibly miftake the meaning of
them

them, yet the grammarians of thofe days did make a fhift to explain, that the words, if need be, did relate as well to the words every year once, as to the words more often; and fo, by this grammatical whimfey of theirs, have made this ftatute to fignify juft nothing at all. For this reafon, my Lords, in the 36th year of the fame king's reign, a new act of parliament was made, in which thofe unfortunate words, if need be, are left out and that act of parliament relating to Magna Charta and other ftatutes, made for the publick good. " Item, For maintenance of thefe articles and fta- " tutes, and the redrefs of divers mifchiefs and " grievances, which daily happen, a parliament " fhall be holden every year; as at other time " was ordained by another ftatute." Here now, my Lords, there is not left the leaft colour or fhadow for any miftake; for it is plainly declared, that the kings of England muft call a parliament once within a year; and the reafons why we are bound to do fo, are plainly fet down, namely, " For the maintenance of Magna Charta, and " other ftatutes of the fame importance, and for " preventing the mifchiefs and grievances which " daily happen."

The queftion then remaineth, Whether thefe ftatutes have been fince repealed by any other ftatutes or no? The only ftatutes I ever heard mentioned for that, are the two triennial bills, the one made in the laft King's, and the other in this King's reign. The triennial bill in the laft King's reign was made for the confirmation of the two above-mentioned ftatutes of Edward III. For Parliaments having been omitted to be called every

2

year

year according to thofe ftatutes, a ftatute was
made in the laft King's reign, to this purpofe;
" That if the King fhould fail of calling a Parlia-
" ment, according to thefe ftatutes of Edward III.
" then, the third year the people fhould meet of
" themfelves without any writs at all, and choofe
" their Parliament-men." This way of the peo-
ples choofing Parliament-men of themfelves being
thought difrefpectful to the King, a ftatute was
made in this laft Parliament, which repealed the
triennial bill; and after the repealing claufe
(which took notice only of the triennial bill made
in the laft King's reign,) there was in this ftatute
a paragraph to this purpofe: " That becaufe by
" the ancient ftatutes of this realm, made in the
" reign of Edward III. Parliaments are to be held
" very often, it fhould be enacted, that within
" three years after the determination of that
" prefent Parliament, Parliaments fhould not be
" difcontinued above three years at moft, and
" fhould be holden oftener if need required."
There have been feveral half kind of arguments
drawn out of thefe triennial bills againft the ftatutes of Edward III. which I confefs I could never
remember, nor indeed thofe that urged them to
me ever durft own: for they always laid their
faults upon fomebody elfe, like ugly foolifh children, whom, becaufe of their deformity and want
of wit, the parents are afhamed of, and fo turn
them out on the parifh.

But, my Lords, let the arguments be what they
will, I have this fhort anfwer to all that can be
wrefted out of thefe triennial bills, " That the
" firft triennial bill was repealed before the mat-
" ter

" ter now difputed of was in queftion, and the
" laft triennial bill will not be in force till the
" queftion be decided, that is, till the parliament
" is diffolved." The whole matter, my Lords,
is reduced to this fhort dilemma; either the kings
of England are bound by the acts above-mentioned
of Edward III. or elfe the whole government of
England by Parliaments, and by the law above,
is abfolutely at an end: for if the kings of England have power, by an order of theirs, to invalidate an act made for the maintenance of Magna
Charta, they have alfo power, by an order of theirs,
to invalidate Magna Charta itfelf; and if they have
power, by an order of theirs, to invalidate the ftatute itfelf, *De Tallagio non concedendo* ; then they
may not only, without the help of a parliament,
raife money when they pleafe ; but alfo take away
any man's eftate when they pleafe, and deprive
every one of his liberty or life as they pleafe.

This, my Lords, I think is a power that no
judge nor lawyer will pretend the kings of England have ; and yet this power muft be allowed
them, or elfe we that are met here this day cannot act as a parliament. For we are now met by
virtue of the laft prorogation, and that prorogation is an order of the King's, point-blank, contrary
to the two acts of Edward III. For the acts fay,
" That a Parliament fhall be holden once within
" a year; and the prorogation faith, a parliament
" fhall not be held within a year, but fome
" months after ;" and this (I conceive) is a plain
contradiction, and confequently that the prorogation is void. Now, if we cannot act as a parlia-
i   ment,

ment, by virtue of the laſt prorogation, I beſeech your Lordſhips, by virtue of what elſe can we act? Shall we act by virtue of the king's proclamation? Pray, my Lords, how ſo? Is a proclamation of more force than a prorogation? Or if a thing that hath been ordered the firſt time be not valid, doth the ordering it the ſecond time make it good in law? I have heard indeed, that two negatives make an affirmative; but I never heard before that two nothings ever made any thing.

Well, but how then are we met? Is it by our own adjournment? I ſuppoſe no body has the confidence to ſay that: Which way then is it? Do we meet by accident? That I think may be granted; but an accidental meeting can no more make a parliament, than an accidental clapping a crown upon a man's head can make a king. There is a great deal of ceremony required to give a matter of that moment a legal ſanction. The laws have repoſed ſo great a truſt, and ſo great a power in the hands of a parliament, that every circumſtance relating to the manner of their electing, meeting and proceeding, is looked after with the niceſt circumſpection imaginable. For this reaſon, the king's writs, about the ſummons of parliament, are to be iſſued out *verbatim*, according to the form preſcribed by the law, or elſe that parliament is void and null. For the ſame reaſon, if a parliament, ſummoned by the King's writ, do not meet the very ſame day that it is ſummoned to meet upon, that parliament is void and null : and, by the ſame reaſon, if parliaments be not legally adjourned, *de die in diem*, thoſe parliaments muſt be alſo void and null.

Oh ! but fome fay, there is nothing in the two acts of Edward III. to take away the King's power of prorogation, and therefore the prorogation is good. My Lords, under favour, this is a very grofs miſtake ; for, pray examine the words of the act : the act fays, " A parliament ſhall be holden " once a year ;" now to whom can thefe words be directed, but to them who are to call a parliament ? And who are they but the Kings of England ? It is very true, this does not take away the King's power of proroguing parliaments ; but it moſt certainly limits it to be within a year. Well then, but it is ſaid again, if that prorogation be null and void, then things are juſt as they were before, and therefore the parliament is ſtill in being. My Lords, I confefs there would be fome weight in this, but for one thing, which is, that not one word of it is true ; for if, when the King had prorogued us, we had taken no notice of the prorogation, but had gone on like a parliament, and had adjourned ourſelves *de die in diem* ; then, I confefs, things had been juſt as they were before : but fince upon the prorogation we went away, and took no care of ourſelves for our meeting again, if we cannot meet and act by virtue of that prorogation, there is an impoſſibility of our meeting and acting any other way. One may as properly fay, that a man that is killed by affault is ſtill alive, becaufe he was killed unlawfully, as that the parliament is ſtill alive becaufe the prorogation was unlawful. The next argument that thofe are reduced to who would maintain this to be yet a parliament is, that the parliament is prorogued

rogued *fine die*, and therefore the king may call them again by proclamation. In the firft part of this propofition I fhall not only agree with them, but alfo do them the favour to prove, that it is fo in the eye of the law, which I never heard they have yet done. For the ftatutes fay, "That a " parliament fhall be holden once within a year?" and the prorogation having put them off till a day without the year, and confequently excepted againft by the law, that day, in the eye of the law, is no day at all, that is, *fine die :* and the prorogation might as well have put them off till fo many months after dooms-day; and then I think nobody would have doubted, but that had been a very fufficient difiolution.

Befides, my lords, I fhall defire your lordfhips to take notice, that in former times the ufual way of diffolving parliaments was to difmifs them *fine die* ; for the king, when he diffolved them, ufed to fay no more, but that he defired them to go home, till he fent for them again, which is a dif- miffion *fine die*. Now if there were forty ways of diffolving parliaments, if I can prove this parlia- ment has been diffolved by any one of them, I fuppofe there is no great need of the other thirty nine. Another thing, which they much infift upon, is that they have found out a precedent in queen Elizabeth's time, when a parliament was once prorogued three days beyond a year. In which I cannot chufe but obferve, that it is a very great confirmation of the value and efteem all people ever had of the forementioned acts of Edward III. fince, from that time to this, there can but one

predecent be found for the proroguing a parliament above a year, and that was but for three
days neither. Besides, my lords, this precedent
is of a very odd kind of nature; for it was in the
time of a very great plague, when every body of a
sudden was forced to run away one from another,
and so, being in haste, had not leisure to calculate
well the time of the prorogation; though the ap-
pointing it to be within three days of the year is
an argument to me, that their design was to keep
within the bounds of the acts of parliament. And
if the mistake had been taken notice of in queen
Elizabeth's time, I make no question but she
would have given a lawful remedy.

Now I beseech your lordships, what more can be
drawn from the shewing this precedent, but only
that, because once upon a time a thing was done
illegally, therefore your lordships should do so
again now? Though, my lords, under favour,
ours is a very different case from theirs; for this
precedent they mention was never taken notice of,
and all lawyers will tell you, that a precedent that
passes *sub silentio* is of no validity at all, and will
never be admitted into any judicial court, where
it is pleaded. Nay, Judge Vaughan says in his
reports, " That in cases which depend upon fun-
" damental principles, from which demonstra-
" tions may be drawn, millions of precedents are
" to no purpose." Oh! but say they, you must
think prudentially of the inconveniencies which
will follow upon it: For if this be allowed, all
those acts which were made in that session of parliament will be then void. Whether that be so or
no,

no, I fhall not now examine ; but this I will pretend to fay, that no man ought to pafs for a pru-
dential perfon who only takes notice of the inconveniencies of one fide. It is the part of a wife man
to examine the inconveniences of both fides, to
weigh which are the greateft, and to be fure to
avoid them. And, my lords, to that kind of examination I willingly fubmit this caufe ; for I prefume it will be eafy for your lordfhips to judge,
which of thefe two will be of the moft dangerous
confequence to the nation ; either to allow, that
the ftatutes made in that particular feffion in
queen Elizabeth's time are void, (which may
eafily be confirmed by a lawful parliament,) or to
lay it down for a maxim, " That the kings of
" of England, by a particular order of theirs,
" have power to break all the laws of England
" when they pleafe."

And, my lords, with all the duty we owe to his
majefty, it is no difrefpect to him to fay, that his
majefty is bound up by the laws of England ; for
the great King of heaven and earth, God Almighty himfelf, is bound by his own decrees : and
what is an act of parliament, but a decree of the
king made in the moft folemn manner it is poffible for him to make it, that is, with the confent
of the lords and commons: it is plain then, in
my opinion, that we are no more a parliament ;
and I humbly conceive, your lordfhips ought to
give God thanks for it, fince it has thus pleafed
him, by his providence, to take you out of a condition, wherein you muft have been entirely ufe-
lefs to his majefty, to yourfelves, and the whole

R 2
nation:

nation : for, I do befeech your lordſhips, if nothing of this I have urged were true, what honourable excuſe could we find, for our acting again, with the houſe of commons ? Except we could pretend ſuch an exquiſite art of forgetfulneſs, as to avoid calling to mind all that paſſed between us the laſt ſeſſions ; and unleſs we could have alſo a faculty of teaching the ſame art to the whole nation. What opinion could they have of us, if it ſhould hap-pen, that the very ſame men, who were ſo earneſt the laſt ſeſſion for having the houſe of commons diſſolved, when there was no queſtion of their lawful ſitting, ſhould be now willing to join with them again, when without queſtion they are diſ-ſolved ?

Nothing can be more dangerous to a king or a people, than that the laws ſhould be made by an aſſembly, of which there can be a doubt, whether they have power to make laws or no : and it would be in us inexcuſable, if we ſhould over-look this danger, ſince there is for it ſo eaſy a re-medy, which the law requires, and which all the nation longs for.

The calling a new parliament it is, that only can put his majeſty into a poſſibility of receiving ſupplies; that can ſecure your lordſhips the ho-nour of ſitting in this houſe like peers, and of be-ing ſerviceable to your king and country; and that can reſtore to all the people of England their undoubted rights of chooſing men frequently to repreſent their grievances in parliament; without this, all we can do would be in vain; the nation

may

may languish a while but muft perish at laft: we should become a burden to ourfelves, and a prey to our neighbours. My motion therefore to your lordfhips fhall be, that we humbly addrefs ourfelves to his majefty, and beg of him, for his own fake, as well as for the people's fake, to give us fpeedily a new parliament; that fo we may unanimoufly, before it is too late, ufe our utmoft endeavours for his majefty's fervice, and for the fafety, the welfare, and the glory of the Englifh nation.

** *Whilft another was fpeaking, the duke of Buckingham took a pen, and writ this fyllogifm; and then appealed to the bifhops, whether it were not a true fyllogifm; and to the judges, whether the propofitions were not true in law.*

THE SYLLOGISM.

IT is a maxim in the law of England, that the kings of England are bound up, by all the ftatutes made *pro bono publico,* that every order or direction of theirs contrary to the fcope, and full intent of any fuch ftatute, is void and null in law.

But, the laft prorogation of the parliament was an order of the king's contrary to an act of king Edward III. made for the greateft common good, *viz.* The maintenance of all the ftatutes of England, and for the prevention of the mifchiefs and grievances which daily happen.

Therefore

Therefore, the laſt prorogation of parliament is void and null in law.

* _Spoken by the duke in the houſe of lords_, February 15th, 1676. _For which he was ſent to the tower._

Suffering is ſweet when honour doth adorn it.
Who ſlights revenge? not he that fears, but ſcorns it.

F I N I S.

CONTENTS OF VOL. I.

DIALOGUE.

CONTENTS.

DIALOGUE.